Praise for The Year of Return

"Fast-paced and fantastical, Akotowaa delivers a chilling reimagination of contemporary times brimming with commentary on the Year of Return Blackness and Africanness."

—Kobby Ben Ben, author

"A moving and timely perspective on one of the greatest horrors in human history. Ofori presents ancient and recent events in a startlingly original take about our responsibilities to our past, our present, and our future."

—R.S.A. Garcia, Locus, Sturgeon, Nebula and IGNYTE Award finalist

"Akotowaa's The Year of Return is a moving story weaving history, family ties, and found community into a unique tapestry. It seamlessly pulls the past into the present, bringing ancestors and descendants together, and forcing to the surface the consequences of injustices long committed. This book also gives closure, honor, and vengeance to a people long lost to the ocean's depths. At the same time, it reveals that no one is ever truly lost or forgotten as long as their stories are carried through time. Akotowaa accomplishes this without holding back, without being delicate, and in utter defiance. She presents the lived experiences of our ancestors in its rawest, most authentic form. The Year of Return is a remembrance, an unearthing, and a worthy piece of storytelling."

—Oghenechovwe Donald Ekpeki. Nebula, Locus, Otherwise, British, World Fantasy award winner, Hugo, British Science Fiction & NAACP Image award finalist.

"Ivana Akotowaa Ofori's THE YEAR OF RETURN is a haunting, darkly evocative tale of the ghosts of the past, delivering a harrowing vision of history's undeniable grasp on the present and the future alike."

—Kevin Wabaunsee, assistant editor at Escape Pod, former managing editor of the SFWA

"Ivana Akotowaa Ofori's debut novella is a riveting tale of vengeance centuries in the making. Unease seeps into the psyche from the first pages and lingers long after the story is over. Ofori's voice – fresh, distinct, and unpretentious

– creates a disquieting sense that everything that happens on the page could happen in the real world tomorrow. Yet *The Year of Return* is not just a creepy, cautionary tale or a clever comment on how the evils of history mar the present. It's a nuanced exploration of collective grief, collective responsibility and collective amnesia. It is a call to action, grounded in actual events and all-too familiar characters. Expect exciting things from Ivana Akotowaa Ofori – she is certain to deliver."

—Cheryl S. Ntumy, author of "The Way of Baa'gh" in *Mothersound* and *Songs for the Shadows*

"The Year of Return," the debut novella from Ivana Akotowaa Ofori, is fast paced and thought-provoking. It does a fantastic job of unearthing the roots of the ills in Ghana and the world as we know it. A thoroughly satisfying read."

—Ayesha Harruna Attah

The Year of Return

Ivana Akotowaa Ofori

Android Press

Published by Android Press
Eugene, Oregon
www.android-press.com

ISBN: 978-1958121832

Cover art by Justine Norton-Kertson and Henry Desouza Nelson

For the ancestors.

Contents

Acknowledgements

This work would never have existed, especially not in its current form, without the contributions of those who came before me, those who worked and lived alongside me, those who nurtured me intellectually, and those who helped hone my craft.

I am indebted to several of the professors of the Claremont Colleges in California, most of whom teach in the Africana Studies department. Professors Maryan Soliman, Makhroufi Ousmane Traoré, Marie-Denise Shelton, Eric Hurley, Thomas Koenigs, and especially Rita Roberts, whose class introduced me to the work of Stephanie E. Smallwood, which sparked the idea for this story.

I completed much of the work for this novella during the 2022 West African Writers residency at the Library of Africa and the African Diaspora (LOATAD) in Accra. Thank you to its founder, Sylvia Arthur, as well as all the caretakers who ensured the writers were well cared for. Thank you, Seth Avusuglo, for being everywhere at once, and to Sarpong Osei Asamoah. I owe so much to my fellow residents, for their time and care during workshops: Gabriel Awuah-Mainoo, Immaculata Abba, and Araba Ofori-Acquah, and to our phenomenal workshop facilitator, Elizabeth Johnson.

My dear friend and incredible fellow writer, Fui Can-Tamakloe, you will always be my favorite first reader. Thank you for your kind words and critical eye. Thank you, Denzel Owoo, for your love through the peaks and valleys of this process.

Thank you to my agent, Bieke van Aggelen, and my publisher, Justine Norton-Kertson, for believing so strongly in this story. Two editors have been instrumental: Caitlin Farley at the Van Aggelen literary agency, and Somto Ihezue at Android Press. Thank you for everything you have done for me, both on and off the pages of this novella. Thank you to Henry Desouza Nelson, for your generosity and your design genius.

This work is for the people of African descent everywhere, past, present, and future. I will never have adequate words to thank the ancestors who lived through horrors told and unknown. To them, I offer my work itself. Thank you also to my political, creative, and intellectual ancestors, who believed in and embodied Pan-Africanism, hope, and liberation, including Kwame Nkrumah, Maya Angelou, Thomas Sankara, W.E.B. du Bois, and many more.

Thank you to God, my source and my strength.

Chapter 1

I stood alone on a bailey by a row of cannons overlooking the sea. Nasty, rusting artillery aside, I had a lovely view. Water bluer than blue, interrupted by bright white sea foam; earthy rocks coated with green moss protruding from the shallow seabed; the horizon line separating the blue of the ocean from the blue of the sky.

"Ugh, I can just *feel* the spirits of my ancestors in this place!" A voice behind me effused, in an accent that dripped of Brooklyn, breaking the spell of the view.

Faster than I could control it, my face twisted into something between a grimace and a smirk. Thankfully, I was still facing the sea, my expression hidden from the tourists behind me.

I looked down in shame. All the years of trying to unlearn the reflexive snubbing of African Americans that I'd picked up from my mother, and still so little progress?

But my irritation—and not necessarily at the tourist—was just as challenging to quell. I was sure this sort of reaction was what the Ghanaian government was trying to capitalize on, which made the Year of Return initiative feel much more disingenuous. Unethical, even.

Before college, I'd spent my whole life in Ghana, and nobody had even mentioned the year 1619 in my presence. Suddenly, on its 400th anniversary, the government was marketing itself as if nothing weighed heavier on the hearts of our leaders than the violent dispersal of Black people from Africa. It felt like a weird publicity stunt designed to make money off people who earned in dollars. I might have found it amusing if I wasn't worried about how many Americans were buying into it. The initiative felt even more like a scam now that it was December—the climax of the commemorative year and peak holiday season.

You're being cynical, Adwapa, I admonished myself. *Just like your mother.*

Every time I heard the words, "Year of Return," I had to suppress a groan. But here I was at Cape Coast Castle anyway, because my friends had flown down with me from the US to visit my country, and they wouldn't leave without this quintessential experience.

I had already done two Ghanaian slave castle tours in my twenty-six years of living and had no intentions of making that three. I was content to loiter around the open-air spaces of the castle while my friends completed their guided tour.

It occurred to me that I hadn't taken a single picture since I'd come up here, having been lost in my head until the Brooklynite's interruption. But the scene before me was too beautiful to leave without capturing. I reached for my phone.

No sooner had the imitation shutter click sounded than I felt a shiver crawl through my body. I could have sworn the temperature dropped several degrees in mere seconds. And yet, my shiver had not been one of cold. It was the kind of chill you got when you were convinced death was waiting to pop out at you from within the shadows.

I looked around, trying to see if anyone else had sensed the atmospheric shift, but I was the only one paying attention to the sea. Unsettled, I returned my gaze to the water—and nearly dropped my phone.

There was an object in the distance: a vaguely human figure floating upright above the waves, its brown tint contrasting with the blues of the water and horizon.

It wasn't just the sight of it that shocked me. It was the sudden conviction that this thing, whatever it was, was the source of all my discomfort. The more I looked at it, the more nauseous I became.

"Hey, Dwaps, you good?"

I jumped at Charlene's voice and whirled around to find her, Randy, and Oneisha approaching me, freshly out of their dungeon tour.

"You look like you've seen a ghost," Charlene added.

I forced myself to focus on my best friend's face—her wide deep-set eyes, her golden-brown skin with almost orange undertones—to banish the image of the figure on the sea.

A few moments too late, I snorted back at her, "*I* look like I've seen a ghost? You're the one who just stepped out of a real-life haunted house."

Charlene shrugged. "Eh... Touché."

"So..." I drawled, spreading my attention between all three of my friends. "How was the tour?"

"It was great," said Randy. His pinched face begged to differ. All the color had drained from his cheeks.

"Don't lie to her just because she's our host," Charlene admonished.

I half-expected Randy to defend himself, but he'd become preoccupied with Oneisha. He wrapped one arm tightly around her. Oneisha herself stood as still as a statue, eyes open but empty, as if she'd gone somewhere and left her body behind.

It wasn't until we were all back in our rented Prado, driving away from the Cape Coast Castle, that Oneisha began to bawl like a child awoken from a nightmare.

I was so startled that I nearly hit the brakes right in the middle of the road.

A glance into the rearview mirror showed me Oneisha folded protectively into her boyfriend's arms, trembling and sobbing against him. Her huge, curly brown wig almost obscured his mouth, but I was just able to read his lips: *Keep going*. And so I did.

Oneisha was still crying by the time I pulled into the car park of the Golden Glow Beach Resort—our residence for the weekend. It was at least five more minutes before she felt composed enough to leave the car.

As for me, I was still secretly mulling over whatever I thought I'd seen over the water and wondering why anxiety was gathering in my chest like a brewing storm.

I made my way along the edges of the hotel room, flinging all the curtains as wide open as I possibly could. I still hoped that the sunlight would drive away my residual chills.

Charlene slouched in our room's armchair, her absurdly long goddess locs spilling all over her torso. She didn't say a word about my strange behavior, and that was how I knew just how much that tour had affected her. Gone was the forced levity she'd displayed back at the castle. Now, this woman who always had a snarky comment ready at the tip of her tongue just watched me, listless, as I fought my war against the shadows.

The morning's tour hadn't been Charlene's first experience of this kind. But visiting a slave castle wasn't like getting chickenpox; you didn't go through it once and then face all subsequent exposure with immunity. I had thought opting out of today's tour would preserve my emotional health, but that strange illusion and all its effects had messed me up almost as badly as Charlene looked.

Once the room was awash with daylight, I took a deep breath and perched myself on the edge of my bed.

The bathroom door that connected mine and Charlene's room to Oneisha and Randy's slowly swung open. Oneisha emerged through it, cradling a mist diffuser in her palms. She had probably curated the essential oil blend within it long in advance.

Charlene's eyes trailed Oneisha as she plugged the diffuser into the wall. Water vapor began to fill the air with several scents I struggled to identify, besides sage. Charlene cocked an eyebrow at me when she thought Oneisha wasn't looking. She didn't yet understand that Oneisha never needed to look.

Oneisha lowered herself into a cross-legged position on the floor with her back against the wall. She looked so self-possessed that it was hard to tell that she'd just been crying. Her face may have been a little puffier than usual, but that was inconsequential; she couldn't help but look impossibly gorgeous at all times. With skin as deep as dark roast coffee and something vaguely Sudanese about her face, she could have been the poster child for African beauty.

She tipped her head back, closed her eyes, and inclined her chin ever so slightly in Charlene's direction before she said, "Don't worry; there's nothing wrong with how you feel. It doesn't get easier just because you grew up."

Charlene's already large eyes widened as her eyebrows

scrunched together and her lip curled to the left. "What?" she blurted, clearly having understood Oneisha's words perfectly.

"You were taken on a tour as a child," Oneisha replied patiently. "You thought you would handle it better as an adult, but there's no reason to be ashamed of how much it made you feel."

Charlene's eyes zapped back to mine, full of alarm. I had tried many times to explain that it was normal for Oneisha to know things she'd never been told. This was a woman who could read people's internal affairs as if they were being advertised on flashing neon signs. Her awareness of the unseen and the unspoken was borderline invasive, sometimes comical. She could walk into a room of strangers and identify, with complete accuracy, who had slept with whom, no matter how far apart they stood from each other, and that was close to the least of her abilities. But Charlene was not easily convinced.

"By the end of this week, babe, you will be a believer," I said to her.

"Nah." Charlene shook her head. "Nah, I must have said something to tip her off."

I nearly chuckled, but this was a conversation the two of us could continue in private.

"How are you guys feeling now?" I asked.

Quietly, Oneisha replied, "We will sit with this. Reckon with it. Talk through it. But first..."

As if on cue, the bathroom door swung open again to reveal Randy maneuvering his way through with his hips and elbows. His arms were occupied with balancing a tray of four identical, icy cocktails.

"We will drink," Oneisha finished.

Charlene's entire body relaxed at once. Oneisha was finally speaking a language they both understood.

As Randy passed the drinks around to each of us, I thought to myself for the hundredth time that he was far too much of a sweetheart to look this much like a player. It wasn't just the gallery of black ink tattoos on his arms, neck, and torso; it was also the short, raven-black hair, the thickset eyebrows, and the slender sharpness of his body that invoked a sense of danger that Randy's personality would never be able to live up to.

He served me first, then Charlene. Finally, Oneisha took a glass from his tray and smiled at him, showing off her distinctive diastema. Randy set his tray down, picked up the last cocktail, and slid down next to her on the floor. In a move practiced enough to have become thoughtless, he slipped his tattoo-sleeved right arm between the wall and her neck, letting his forearm drape casually off her shoulder.

For the next few minutes, my friends and I sat and drank. The coconut water, pineapple juice, and tequila were a good combination. Not surprising, since Randy seemed incapable of making bad decisions.

In the silence, I observed Oneisha, marveling at how well she kept herself together. The dungeon tour had shaken Randy and depressed Charlene, but neither could compare to whatever Oneisha had going on. Even for me, as a young teenager, being in those lightless underground rooms, seeing the blood, sweat, shit, and urine stains on those too-close walls, imagining hundreds and hundreds of people at a time crammed in there, eating in the same place they shat, dying and painfully giving birth on top of each other... It was too much for me and my excitable imagination. And if an ordinary person would shudder at the atmosphere of a slave dungeon, Oneisha, with her spiritual hyper-sensitivity, would shatter,, experiencing the echoes of trauma in real time.

Oneisha was the one to break the silence. Her voice trembled slightly as she said, "I have never, ever been in a place that had such miserable, heart-rending energy."

"Can't argue with that," Charlene muttered.

"All those things the ancestors went through," Oneisha continued. "All those horrible, *horrible* things..." She looked first at Charlene and then at me. I held back a shiver; her eyes told me that she had seen and felt things in that castle that I hoped I never would. "No tour guide's account could ever do those ancestors justice."

"I'm so tempted to order the most expensive thing on the menu and make Randy pay for it," Charlene joked, lazily flipping through her menu.

For lunch today, the four of us had opted for outside seating at the Golden Glow's restaurant.

We'd all been a little too depressed yesterday after the castle to take advantage of anything beyond room service, but today, we were determined to make the most of our last meal in Cape Coast before heading back to Accra. This was my friends' first time in Ghana, and it was important to me that they had an excellent culinary experience.

Oneisha's menu lay closed on the table before her as she sketched on a napkin. She had figured out what she wanted to eat after twenty seconds of browsing through the menu, but the rest of us were having a tough time deciding.

Randy looked up from his menu, cocked a bushy eyebrow at Charlene, and said, "You know what? I'll gladly take you up on that dare. And I have a feeling neither of us will regret it."

Charlene and I exchanged wicked smiles, both impressed but excited for different reasons. Charlene, a few days ago, had found out exactly how much Randy made as a financial quantitative analyst—whatever the hell that was—and had asked him if he was interested in taking on a sugar baby, in Oneisha's presence. I hadn't laughed as hard as Randy had, knowing as I did that Char was at least twenty percent serious. Working in HR wasn't exactly making her millions. As for me, I knew now that any time Randy "had a feeling" about something, it resulted in the best possible experience at the lowest possible cost.

Randy raised his hand to signal a waiter and called out, in an accent that wasn't his own, "Hello, boss!"

A surprised snort ripped out of me at the terrible imitation of Ghanaian culture, which turned into full-blown laughter at the sight of the waiter's face when he saw who was calling.

Randy, to his credit, kept his face perfectly solemn as the waiter came over, pen in hand, ready to take our order.

"Boss," Randy said again, and I had to stop myself from choking. "What's your name?"

"Charles, sir," the waiter replied. The poor man looked so rigid, maybe even a little terrified, and of everyone at the table, he had eyes only for Randy. But Randy had that effect on people; with his dark hair, severe features, and a plethora of tattoos. He looked like he could stab you if you crossed him. The affectation he was putting on for our amusement was certainly not helping poor Mr. Charles.

"Charles," Randy repeated. "What's the most expensive thing on the menu?"

Charles' professional mask slipped for a moment at the unusual question, but he caught himself a second later. "I have to say, maybe the lobster sharing platter, sir. But that's the lunch special for today, so there's a discount. Just for today only."

"Of course there is," I muttered, grinning at Randy.

"That has to be a coincidence," Charlene said.

Oneisha released a single, sharp chortle.

"Believer by the end of the week," I reminded Charlene.

We bantered for a few minutes before our food came, and once it did, all other conversation was forgotten. The jollof was the perfect level of spicy, and the seafood was expertly seasoned. The lobster was expensive even after the discount, but we all agreed it had proved worth every cedi. When the bill arrived, Randy gave Charles a stupidly generous tip and asked him to share it with the Golden Glow's kitchen staff.

Before brunch, we had checked out and packed all our bags into the car. But we were too full to begin our journey back to Accra , so we unrolled a couple of our mats and lounged for a while on the beach, catching a breeze and a hopefully discreet smoke.

"So, my friend," said Charlene, puffing and passing the joint to me. She spoke softly so that only I could hear. "When are you planning to tell me what is doing you?"

I considered pretending not to know what she was on about, but then I sighed. After seven years of being best friends, Charlene knew me too well. We'd met in our first year of college, when we'd been paired as roommates, and ever since then, she'd been able to read me like a book. But I didn't know how to explain my lingering unease, or the apparition that had caused it without sounding raving mad—not even to my best friend. So, instead of a lie, I opted for a half-truth.

"The temperature doesn't feel... normal," I responded carefully.

I must not have spoken quietly enough because Oneisha heard me and said, "It isn't the temperature, Adwapa. It's the vibrations in the atmosphere. The wind is carrying something... Something wild and unexpected."

Charlene rolled her eyes. Honestly, I couldn't blame her for her low Oneisha tolerance. I'd been just as bad—even worse—when I'd first met Oneisha and heard her spiels about energies, crystals, and Black divinity. But I'd had three years of friendship and proximity to get used to it (Oneisha and I had met, and both lived in California), whereas Charlene had only met Oneisha twice before this trip, on brief visits from the East Coast to see me.

"Something wild in the winds, eh?" Charlene said. "Let me see if I can catch a whiff of it too."

"Oh, Jesus," I groaned, knowing that Charlene was about to do something both rude and hilarious.

Sure enough, she rose with all the drama of a self-important monarch, shedding her beach cover-up and leaving herself in only her booty shorts and crop top. Inhaling deeply, she stretched her hands to her sides as if to catch the wind, then twirled a little with her head tilted back. She looked high as hell—not to mention utterly ridiculous—and I couldn't stop myself from giggling.

I almost thought it was part of the act when she abruptly dropped her hands, exclaiming, "Ya Allahi, what the hell is that?"

The rest of us scrambled to our feet and squinted toward Charlene's gaze.

"No fucking way," Randy muttered.

Oneisha grabbed his arm—and mine—and trembled, muttering curses and prayers under her breath. The oxymoron would have been hilarious if the atmosphere hadn't suddenly become so intense.

The same unnatural chill that I'd felt back at the castle seeped into my marrow again, but several times stronger. Knowing now that my friends could all see what I saw either meant that I wasn't crazy or that all of us were. Nobody said another word as we gawked at the horizon, waiting, perhaps, for the visions to disappear.

They remained.

Impossibly, they remained, and with every second, terror spread through my veins like somebody was draining my body of blood and replacing it with ice.

Finally, after about a minute, Charlene asked, in a tremulous whisper, "Adwapa, what the hell is this weed laced with?"

Music played for the first few minutes of the drive back to Accra, but I, for one, heard none of it over the static in my brain. My friends were just as shaken, Charlene staring straight ahead in the shotgun seat, Randy and Oneisha as still as statues in the back.

It was the weed, I tried to convince myself. *It was just the weed. A group hallucination.*

Slowly, my muscles began to unclench, and I relaxed further back into the driver's seat, surrendering to the high. Little by little, laughter began to bubble up and out of me, giggles that quickly progressed into guffaws so forceful I had to pull over and park the car. Just before it got so bad that I couldn't breathe, Charlene joined in, followed soon by Randy. Even Oneisha eventually released a few nervous giggles, if only at the ludicrousness of being parked in the middle of nowhere with three other stoned adults.

Because who the hell—including ourselves—would ever believe that we'd just seen a group of stark-naked men, women, and children marching on the surface of the sea toward the shores of Ghana?

The TV was on in my mother's living room, but I wasn't watching it. I lay stretched out on the couch, staring at my phone screen and trying not to think about the apparitions. Charlene was upstairs, showering away the beach sand. We had left Randy and Oneisha at their hotel in the Airport area with the Prado—since it was technically Randy's car rental—and then we'd Ubered back to my house.

My mother emerged from the kitchen, her sew-in weave wrapped in her usual scarf, and made her way to her favorite armchair. I acknowledged her with a half-smile, but the smirk she returned was not nearly as good-willed.

"So you've finished reliving your friend's ancient history?" she sneered.

Anger exploded in my chest, and it took everything to restrain my tongue.

As if Cudjo Lewis hadn't lived well into the twentieth century, hadn't died less than three decades before my mother herself was born!

My *friend's* ancient history, as if Ghanaians weren't Black too. As if all the forts and castles still standing in this country had absolutely nothing to do with us. Or perhaps it was the "African" in "African American" that she was having trouble understanding.

My friend. She couldn't even give Oneisha the dignity of saying her name.

My mother had disliked Oneisha from their first interaction, just after we'd gotten out of baggage claim at Kotoka a few days earlier. Of course, Oneisha had read my mother's aura, or whatever she called it, but if there was one thing about Oneisha, it was that she would be herself in every room, no matter what people thought of her. She'd spoken about how happy she was to finally be "in the motherland," her gratitude at the opportunity to "reclaim her identity," and the symbolism of how she, a descendant of enslaved people, had made the trip to the region where her ancestors were taken from.

While Oneisha spoke, my mother had taken in her colorful dashiki dress and wax print headscarf, her dangling round earrings made of beads in the colors of the South African flag. One look at my mother's face at that moment, and I knew exactly what she thought: that Oneisha was confirmation of every awful stereotype she'd ever had about Black Americans.

My mother believed African Americans were "obsessed" with race and with all the oppression that she claimed was "long behind us." Needless to say, she'd never quite forgiven me for switching my undergrad major from Economics to Africana Studies. "So you went all the way to America for me to pay white people to teach you about where you just came from? Is this how you are wasting your Ivy League education?" she'd asked me. And although she was fine with my chosen profession as a journalist, she thought the stories I covered—stories from the Black community in America that mainstream news often sidelined—were irrelevant.

Oneisha had generally avoided my mother since it was immediately clear they would never be comfortable around each other.

With a truly Herculean effort, I decided to let my mother's comment about "my friend's ancient history" slide. It wasn't as if our previous arguments on the subject had gone anywhere.

In an attempt to distract myself, I opened Twitter. And

for the second time in as many days, I nearly dropped my phone.

I must have cried out, because my mother snapped to alertness, back straight and eyes sharp as she barked, "Dɛɛn na asi?"

"The people," I wheezed. "Walking on water."

Others were seeing them too. Hazy clips were circulating on Twitter, and though none of the apparitions in the videos were the same ones I'd seen, they had the same things in common: they were all Black, all naked, and all blatantly defying the laws of physics.

My mother gave a long, exasperated suck of her teeth and relaxed into her armchair once more. "Oh, that thing? Mtchew," she sucked again. "I saw that nonsense on my WhatsApp platform. It's a hoax."

She said it with so much confidence that I almost believed her. But... "I've *seen* some, Mummy," I said. "When we were at Cape Coast—"

"Have you been smoking wee?" she asked sharply.

My mouth snapped into a grim line. Dr. Florence Mensah was far from a religious fanatic, but she did hold strong opinions about what she termed "wayward behavior." From experience, I knew that once "wee" came up, the only prudent course of action was to terminate the conversation immediately.

Without another word, I got up and went to my room.

Charlene and I lay on my bed, peering at my laptop screen with all the intensity we'd have dedicated to a psychological thriller. But we were watching something much more stressful: my constantly refreshing Twitter timeline.

In just a few hours, the rumble on the internet surrounding the spectral figures had turned into a full-blown virtual earthquake, as people uploaded more and more media from the towns of Cape Coast and Elmina.

Many of the videos had been captured by fishermen, but a few were starting to emerge from locals and tourists alike. A few of the apparitions had made it onto the shores and even into the villages. The internet was going crazy.

"This can't be real, Adwapa," Charlene groaned. "We were just high!"

"Well, smartphone cameras don't get high," I replied, scrolling further down.

Ghana Twitter didn't know how to take anything seriously. Jokes were being quoted and retweeted all over the timeline, some about the apparitions' nudity, some about the power of Ghallywood's video editors, but most of them farcical references to that most legendary of West African deities. The right-hand column on my screen indicated that #MamiWatasChildren was the top trend in the region.

To some extent, I understood how social media could afford to draw comedic value from this. It was so much easier when all you were interacting with was a video someone else had shot. You couldn't feel the visceral fear and cold-ness accompanying those visions through a screen. You couldn't just imagine the kind of terror that made you want to pee yourself. You had to *be there*.

The madness refused to slow down. I could have kept scrolling all night if Charlene hadn't declared, "Enough," just before 2:15 a.m. and forced my laptop shut. I had to blink moisture back into my eyes.

When I woke up in the morning, the first thing I reached for was my phone. I barely registered the date on my lock screen—24th December, Christmas Eve—before I jabbed at the Twitter icon.

I cursed loudly.

Charlene raised her head with a start, eyes snapping open. "What? What's happening?"

"They've reached Accra!" I said.

Some Jamestown fishermen had gotten the shock of their lives this dawn, and they'd come online to tell their followers. Likewise, some vacationers staying in beach ho-tels along the Labadi coast were making entire threads describing how it felt to encounter these beings. Their accounts sounded similar to what my friends and I had gone through at Cape Coast.

The humor that had first surrounded the #Mami-WatasChildren trend was quickly being eclipsed by fear and horror.

Ignoring the fact that it was way too early to be reaching out to anyone, especially on Christmas Eve, I called Oneisha on speaker. As usual, it felt like she answered before the dial tone even sounded.

"Hey, are you guys up?" I asked. "We have a lot to talk about. I was thinking—"

"You'll be here within the hour, and we'll be ready," Oneisha interrupted.

"Great. See you then."

When I looked up, Charlene was frowning at me with that look which meant her brain was doing some heavy-duty computing. "She knew you wanted to come over before you said you wanted to." Without waiting for my response, she barreled on, "But that's probably because you called her at bloody seven in the morning, and there's no reason for anyone to be calling anybody at that time unless you're late for an appointment, or they need to see you immediately."

"Charlene," I said solemnly. "You are as stubborn as my mother."

Less than an hour later, Charlene and I had joined Oneisha and Randy in their Urban Village Hotel room. The four of us shuffled our gazes between each other and our screens. They all seemed to be looking to me for answers, because I was the Ghanaian, I was the journalist, and I'd called the meeting—but I was just as confused as they were. Our conversation was exasperatingly circular: questions, proposed answers, counter-arguments leading to retractions of initially proposed answers. Rinse and repeat. Through it all, something was pulsing at the back of my mind, straining to break through.

The one thing we all agreed on was that we had really seen, and not merely imagined, those figures at sea. Throughout our discussion, we'd fallen into the habit of calling them "the Coasters," since they only seemed to appear in coastal areas.

"So the next important question is," said Randy, leaning forward as gravely as he might have done in a corporate meeting, "Are these people real people? Are they alive? Are they human?"

"That's *three* questions," Charlene grumbled, frustrated about how little progress we were making but also from the stress of facing things she didn't believe in, yet couldn't explain.

"They're human," Oneisha said softly. "But I'm not entirely sure they're alive."

"But dead people don't walk!" Charlene groaned.

"Fair enough," Randy acknowledged. "But what sorts of living people walk *on water*?"

"Humans infused with divinity might be able to walk on water," Oneisha said.

Charlene groaned, "Oneisha, please." This time, there were no drugs to boost Charlene's tolerance for mystical conjectures.

I wasn't sure what Randy believed, but when it came to spirituality, Charlene and I generally leaned in the same direction. We respected and largely believed in the faiths of our parents—in Char's case, Islam, and in mine, Christianity. But during college, we'd acknowledged to each other that many things about our indigenous African beliefs felt sacred and true as well. Despite our beliefs, though, we hardly ever practiced our faiths. I'd probably describe myself as a lukewarm Africanist Christian, and Charlene was the Muslim equivalent.

Oneisha gave Charlene a long, steady look and then turned her attention on me like I'd feared she would as soon as I heard the last words she'd spoken. "Adwapa, your tradition holds that this is possible."

"It does," I conceded. "Fine. But how would their 'divinity' explain their nudity or their numbers?"

"Christianity does claim that humans were good with nudity before the original sin," Randy pointed out.

Was he insinuating that the Coasters were new, pure, and sinless humans, made from scratch like Adam from Eden's garden soil? As absurd as the current reality was, I didn't know if I could convince my mind to go *that* far.

"*Yieeee!*"

The shriek from Charlene had us all pivoting towards her. She could barely speak as she passed her phone to show us the Tweet that had set her off.

The video she showed us—captured at a beach in Serrekunda—was extraordinarily similar to the ones from here. I might not even have believed this wasn't Ghana if not for the accents and the unfamiliar language of the civilians screaming in the background of the recording.

While I watched the video, something half-sparked in my brain and sputtered out like a car engine straining to life. I couldn't shake the feeling that there was some- thing crucial I should have figured out by now. Ghana and the Gambia. What did we have in common? Both West African. Both former English colonies. Both nations' names start with G? I groaned internally. If I thought any harder, my brain would fracture.

"Alright, guys," said Randy, after watching the video himself. "Hear me out. If these things are showing up in Ghana, and they're showing up in Gambia, it could be a regional phenomenon. Adwapa—" As usual, he butchered my name, emphasizing on the second syllable rather than the last, but at least he'd gotten the general *eh-jwa-PAH* phonetics right. "Do you mind if I modify your search parameters?"

I passed my laptop over to him while Charlene whis- pered, "Since when does Twitter have search parameters?"

When Randy was done doing whatever he did, he had a lot to show us—and much of it was in French.

I had moderate fluency in the language, but it was more than enough to understand the search results. The ap- paritions were being sighted along the Senegalese coast, too! Far fewer were the Tweets from Benin, but there were Coasters there too!

The insistent buzzing in my head became louder than ever. I was sure that the thing that would make everything click was staring me right in the face, but I couldn't see it yet. I sprang up from my lounging position on the hotel room floor and began to pace, muttering fragments of sentences to myself.

"Naked people, naked Black people on the West African coasts... Walking. Walking, but somehow not drowning... Drowning. Water... Walking on water... Jesus. Beach. Coast. Cape Coast. Elmina, Porto Novo... Ports! Ships? Ports and... castles." I stopped dead in my tracks, feeling all the blood drain from my face. "Jesus Christ of Nazareth," I breathed.

Everyone was staring at me, but Oneisha's gaze was the most piercing. "By the fire of Ogun," she whispered, a tremor in her voice.

"Ancestors," she said, right as I gasped, "Slaves!"

Chapter 2

When I woke up the following day, before I'd even opened my eyes, my first words were, "Where's my phone?"

I turned to Charlene, who lay flat on her back, holding my phone above her face and scrolling through my timeline. She didn't even spare me a glance as she replied, "Good morning and Merry Christmas to you, too. I slept great, thanks for asking."

But there was no bite to her sarcasm, and there were dark circles under her eyes.

"Hey, Char, are you okay?"

She finally turned her gaze to me, stress embedded in every line of her face. "Am I *okay*? Dwaps! Just yesterday, you and your voodoo priestess artist friend tried to convince me that we're in the middle of some zombie slave invasion, and now whatever it is has reached Jamaica! How the hell am I supposed to be okay?"

I winced from the verbal onslaught, but then I paused. "Did you just say Jamaica?"

Charlene handed me my phone. Indeed, several nations beyond West Africa were gradually waking up to Coasters on their shores. The birth of Jesus was sidelined as the breaking news of sightings in Jamaica, Haiti, Barbados, Guyana, Suriname, Brazil, and many more disrupted international media's regular programming.

"We have to go to the beach," I breathed.

"You want to get *closer* to those creatures?" Charlene nearly shrieked.

"I want to understand what is going on. Don't you?"

"I just want my sanity back," Charlene complained. "But you're not going to let this go, are you?"

I didn't even have to answer. Charlene was the only one who had known me long enough to recognize the early signs of madness in my eyes. I had a natural tendency towards obsession, and when I wanted answers, I pursued them with all the gravitas of a homicide detective. I called Oneisha and Randy and told them I'd be picking them up much earlier than we'd planned.

My mother was in the kitchen, laying out vegetables and ingredients, when Charlene and I came downstairs.

"Merry Christmas," she greeted, and stopped when she saw we were fully dressed, and I had my car keys in my hand. "Ei, where are you going? I thought you girls were helping me prepare lunch."

My mother had insisted on hosting a Christmas lunch for me and my friends. Of course, she'd made these plans before realizing she had no patience for Oneisha nor any approval to spare for her heavily tattooed boyfriend, but she was far too proud to go back on her word.

"The beach," I said, hugging and pecking my mother quickly on the cheek. "We'll be back in an hour, I promise."

Charlene shrugged apologetically. "Merry Christmas, Auntie Florence."

I caught my mother rolling her eyes at me just before I turned away and made for the front door, Charlene trailing me.

"Don't tell me this has something to do with that hoax on social media," my mother scoffed. "There are better things to do with your time."

"One hour," I called back. The door banged shut behind me.

With all three friends in tow, I pulled up to Old Accra, somewhere off to the side of High Street, and the minute I opened my car door, we were assaulted by noise. It seemed like every church in the neighborhood was holding service at once. Two preachers vied for attention on the same street where I'd parked. They had somehow transported their sound system equipment outside and were screaming into their microphones, switching between Ga and speaking in tongues. I was sure I caught at least one English phrase—"come against the spirits of the devil"—within the cascade of words. The preachers had attracted small crowds of people who listened to them intently, waving their handkerchiefs and muttering fervent amens.

One by one, my friends and I stepped out of my car, and I led the way towards the beach.

There were no boats on the water today, but there were far too many people around for a Christmas morning, especially since the beach just outside Ussher Fort wasn't exactly designed for leisure tourism. Many of those milling around were children; some scruffy, others in church clothes. They'd probably ditched their praying parents on the streets or escaped Sunday School. In any case, I was sure everyone here had come for the same reason.

"Looks like the coast is clear," Charlene joked. Only Randy laughed.

My muscles had been tense from the moment we'd arrived, and the current absence of Coasters wasn't enough to set me at ease.

"Give it a minute," Oneisha countered.

I decided to be brave. I moved forward, closer to the water, passing clusters of people whispering tersely amongst themselves and casting furtive glances towards the sea. They let me through, too apprehensive to get too close themselves.

"Heeey! Hey, kwɛmɔ ei!"

The child's screams set off an avalanche of panic, making Randy jump, but the Coaster hadn't needed the oral announcement. The supernatural chill was enough to catch our attention. Others began to scream and run away from the beach or otherwise back away in terror amidst muttered prayers.

Six more Coasters joined the first, rising out of the sea, their ghostly bodies appearing to form out of darkening ocean mist. I understood now that the haziness I thought I'd seen in all the Twitter videos wasn't haze; it was translucence. The bodies of the Coasters really were more gaseous than solid. But as frightening as their physical presence was, the real terror came from the way they troubled the atmosphere itself, permeating everything with a darkness that clawed its way into one's soul.

I forced myself to stay still, though my heartbeat was hammering in my ears. With Charlene to my left, and Oneisha and Randy to my right, we all had a clear view of the spectacle.

I cleared my throat, pouring the rest of my willpower into trying not to sound like I'd inhaled from a helium balloon. "Oneisha?" I called.

"Yeah?" Her breaths were a bit too deep, but she seemed to be holding up well.

"Can you read their auras?"

She squinted towards the horizon. "It's hard to do that with all the energy from the people around us. The best I can get right now is the color of their presence."

"The color of their presence," Charlene repeated flatly.

"And what does that feel like?" I pressed Oneisha.

"It doesn't feel like life. But it doesn't feel like death either. It's something incomplete."

Ghosts, I thought. A shiver worked its way down my spine, amplifying the icy fear I was already trying to ignore. *These are the ghosts of slaves returned to haunt us for our betrayal. We should have burned all the castles and forts down to the ground. We should have offered sacrifices to every god and God out there and begged to be absolved for our forefathers' sins. We're all going to hell.*

I paused. *No, that's not right*, I thought. *Hell is coming to us.*

I swallowed a lump in my throat and cleared it again. If I wanted answers, I had to keep it together.

"How old do you think they are?" I asked.

Oneisha closed her eyes and breathed in as if her very lungs contained carbon dating equipment. "More than two centuries," came the verdict. "But less than five."

"Audhu billahi min ash shaytanir rajim," muttered Charlene from beside me. I knew that the notions swirling through her mind were the same ones I'd had to suppress mere seconds ago. I reached out for her hand and held it as I continued my interrogation.

"Have you been to any open-casket funerals, Neish?"

"Once or twice."

"And when you look at a body, can you sense the cause of death?"

Oneisha shuddered a little, and that was confirmation enough.

I felt guilty about my next request, but she'd read my energy and already knew what I wanted from her.

"These aren't physical beings, Adwapa," she explained patiently. "They are only echoes. I can't sense the last things their bodies experienced."

"Um, babe?" Randy ventured in a small, hesitant voice, like he wasn't sure he was allowed to speak. "What about their minds?"

I was about to remind him that Oneisha had just complained about not being able to read through all the commotion, but Oneisha raised a finger, signaling me to pause. She turned her head ever-subtly in the direction of one broad-shouldered Coaster man. I glanced back at her. She had her eyes closed, her brows scrunched up, and she looked like she was in pain. After a moment or two, she whispered, just loud enough for the rest of us to hear, "I can't breathe."

Sucker punches to the guts couldn't have winded us any more than those words did. Even Randy couldn't help but wince. Since 2014, those words had become a spell, one with the power to enrage, provoke, and to re-traumatize. Our somatic reactions were automatic and involuntary. It took a little longer to cognitively process what Oneisha had just said, to understand that *those words* had been the Coaster's final thoughts.

Oneisha inclined her head towards another spirit—a woman whose shadow of a body was as lean and muscular as any able-bodied man her age at the peak of health. Her last words had been, "Not here. Not in the water."

By the third reading—another "I can't breathe"—we were all ready for Oneisha to stop.

My eyes began to water, and I heard subtle sniffles from Charlene beside me.

The horror of the Coasters' deaths was entirely at odds with the blankness in their stares, fixed straight ahead as they kept to the rhythms of their various marches. Besides walking in vaguely the same direction, the seven of them didn't seem like a cohesive unit.

My friends and I stood silent for several minutes, simply watching them walk closer and closer to us. No more noise from around or behind us; we might have been the only people left on the beach.

When the first of the seven Coasters stepped onto the shore and carried on walking without even the slightest change in gait, my body urged me to run, but I forced my feet to stay planted and squeezed harder on Charlene's hand.

"Adwapa," Oneisha said, breaking the long silence. I knew that carefully measured tone. It meant she had been trying to find a tactful way to bring up something sensitive. "Would you mind handing Randy your car keys?"

I shifted my gaze to Randy, who looked as surprised

as I did at Oneisha's request, but when I looked back at Oneisha, I immediately understood. Randy would never have said it aloud, but he felt like an intruder. I couldn't blame him; whatever we were experiencing was very sacred and very Black, and Randy, the poor sweetheart, was way out of his depth.

I drew my keys out of my pocket and handed them to Oneisha. She passed them to her boyfriend, who, by this time, had mentally caught up. He graciously accepted the permission to exit.

Sometime after he left, the rest of the Coasters made it to shore as well, each carrying on in a slightly different direction towards inland Accra. They walked on earth as mechanically as they had on water, no bumps or ridges adding any irregularity to their steps.

It took a ton of willpower not to move when one of them was only a few feet away. I found myself holding my breath while examining him. He was tall but scrawny in an unsettling way; I got the sense that it was more the result of starvation than his natural physique. His facial hair was scattered in patches, more haphazard than any beard I'd ever seen, even those of the so-called madmen on the streets of Accra.

But it was his eyes, more than anything, that I could not bear to look into. They were open, but there was nothing in them—no light, no spark, none of the things I now realized I took for granted in any living person's face. That hollowness was almost more heartbreaking than pain. Pain I had seen many times before. But never had I encountered a dead man walking.

I understood, with a sudden, sickening feeling, that this man's eyes had started to look this empty even before the ocean had finally claimed his last breath.

All at once, I couldn't breathe.

I had to leave this place. I was going to throw up right here on the beach and faint into my vomit if I didn't leave. I turned and fled towards my car, barely registering my friends' footsteps behind me.

Tears were streaming recklessly down my face by the time I threw myself into the car. Somewhere in the periphery of my mind, I knew that I'd startled Randy. But I had all but forgotten who I was, where I was, forgotten everything except that hollowness, the feeling of oblivion that had clung to the man who had died of suffering before suffocation had killed him.

Christmas lunch was a civil mess. I was lost in my head, Oneisha was emotionally exhausted, Charlene was undergoing an existential crisis, and try as he might, Randy could not pretend enough cheer for the four of us.

He reached towards the center of our mahogany dining table, where most of the food we'd prepared still sat in pretty glass dishes, barely touched by anyone besides himself and my mother. He scooped out another spoonful of kontomire to add to the remaining yam on his plate.

"This is so good, Dr. Mensah," he said.

"Thank you," my mother replied, without a smile or even the minutest incline in his direction.

On any other day, I'd have called this ampesi excellent; my mother's kontomire was always flavorful and the consistency was just right. Today, however, everything tasted like my tongue had been dipped in ash. It was hard to describe how the proximity to the Coasters had made me feel. I wanted to lay down my clothes for them to walk on. I wanted to kneel at their feet and beg for forgiveness. I wanted to do the impossible—erase the sea from existence, burn every ship on earth as if it could undo what had been done. I wanted to drag the sun down from heaven and present it to them as a gift—anything to bring light back into their hollowed eyes. I felt unworthy to be alive while they were not, and I was willing to do anything I could to recompense for that. I wanted, more than anything, to serve them.

I stared down at my plate, feeling the heat of my mother's glare on my forehead. Her initial frustration at our odd behavior had blossomed into a simmering anger. Each time I spared a glance at her, the set of her mouth betrayed her urge to rant about how foolish we were to have allowed this ridiculous "hoax" to affect us so deeply that we couldn't even enjoy Christmas again.

In my peripheral vision, I saw Oneisha raise her left hand

to stroke the irregular amethyst gemstone she often wore on her neck. My mother caught the movement too. She turned to Oneisha and asked, "Do you celebrate Christmas?"

I looked up then, wary.

"I think Christmas is a lovely holiday that has grown to transcend cultures and faiths," Oneisha replied placidly. "I enjoy the celebration."

"Hm," my mother sniffed. That single syllable set off a bomb of tension, thick as smoke, within the room. For the rest of the meal, it mingled with the gloom and exhaustion the girls and I had brought back from the beach. It remained in the air long after we'd cleared up what was left of the meal into the kitchen.

I placed a final bowl of leftovers into the fridge and joined my friends in the living room. Randy sat alone, so I joined him on the couch opposite Charlene and Oneisha.

Charlene looked like she'd aged five years since waking up this morning. She glanced nervously at Oneisha, sitting beside her with her head back and her eyes closed, perhaps in meditation.

"So. Oneisha," Charlene said, cutting her eyes away again. "You can feel things, eh? Things outside yourself. Sort of like an empath?"

"Mm," Oneisha murmured without moving. "You could use those terms."

Charlene nodded and took a deep, long breath but fumbled even more on her next words. "So, uh... Earlier today, at the beach. You felt... something even stronger than what the rest of us felt."

"I'm a little more sensitive to energies and auras, yeah." What a modest way to put it.

Still, Charlene's face crumpled. "How could you stand it?" she rasped. "How—" She trailed off, blinked back moisture from her eyes, and cleared her throat. "I guess what I'm trying to say is I'm sorry for how I've been treating you. It was rude, and I'm done with it."

Oneisha cracked a tired but genuine smile. "Good. Because you were starting to get on my nerves."

The early morning sunlight filtered through the dining room windows, imposing patterned shadows onto my journal through the curtains. My gel pen stained my hands with blue ink as I scribbled into a messy page full of corrections and cancellations because my hands couldn't keep up with my brain.

It's been six days since I first saw a Coaster at Cape Coast Castle, I wrote. *Now, they are showing up in restaurants, supermarkets, parties, and houses, always marching straight ahead with that fixed determination of theirs. Within and beyond Ghana, some of them have walked long enough to reach the inland cities.*

I still don't know where they're going. Some people say they've seen Coasters walk into houses and then disappear into thin air.

Footsteps creaked on the wooden staircase, interrupting my concentration. I looked up to see my mother in her headscarf and the same clothes she'd had on yesterday. She stood at the bottom of the staircase, preoccupied with something on her phone.

"Ma'akye eh?" she prompted in Twi.

"Good morning, Mummy," I responded.

"I want to start cooking early today, o. What time will you go to the supermarket?"

My pen halted abruptly on a comma, ink soaking into the light paper. I had forgotten entirely about the errand I had agreed to run for her. Oneisha and Randy were already on their way over, and Charlene would be downstairs any minute. The plan was to go back down to the beach—the one place where it was guaranteed there would be Coasters—and see if we could figure out anything more specific about them and why they were here.

My mother met my guilty eyes, and understanding dawned on her. She kissed her teeth loudly and reprimanded me while shuffling into the kitchen. "How many times will I tell you to stop concerning yourself with fake news? Aren't you a journalist? You should know better."

I set my jaw and replaced the cap on my pen. Amidst the sounds of rushing tap water and the clinking of ceramics, my mother continued, "Too many intelligent people are being taken in by this hoax. I'm disappointed. You should hear some of my friends talking about plagues and curses and things. Am I not a Christian too? But I don't indulge in superstitious rubbish."

"Mummy, I'm telling you the visions are real people! The spirits of slaves who drowned in the Atlantic—"

"*Mtcheeeeeeew.*" She drew the sound out long enough to make everything in my vision go red for a second. "Saa w'adamfo no. The American one. She's the one filling your head with such foolishness, isn't it?"

My blood heated up. I opened my mouth.

The gate bell rang.

With considerable effort, I clenched my jaw again and went to let Randy and Oneisha in.

My friends agreed to wait in the car while I ran my errand. I meant to dash to the supermarket, do the shopping, and drop it all back home so we could continue to the beach before the sun got too high in the sky.

The shop was barely ten minutes away, and I had made the journey so many times that I could get there on muscle memory alone. And yet, I had never been so disoriented while driving in Accra.

In just a matter of days, the town had become nearly unrecognizable. Accra, the city of endless December jams, had turned holy. Of course, it was normal that every year, around this time, you could find dozens of "Crossover" billboards and their respective ripoffs, inviting you to usher in the new year with whichever pastors had enough money to erect blown-up images of their faces in the middle of the city. But these were often balanced out by the equally large adverts for Christmas and New Year's beach parties and concerts.

All of those were gone now. It was only two days after Christmas, and between my house and the supermarket, the only billboards I saw bore the words "deliverance," "end of days," and "casting of demons" far too many times to keep track of.

It wasn't just the streets that had become sanctified; it was everything else, too. Beaches had been deserted as people flooded into churches and mosques. Now that all the fishermen had taken an indefinite hiatus, you couldn't get your hands on local seafood to save your life, but if you were looking for an all-night service to attend, you'd be spoiled for choice.

Shopping was a headache. Evangelists prowled the aisles, inviting shoppers to services at their churches, all of which were too obscure for me to have ever heard of. Each swore their pastor knew the real cause of the apparitions and only their prayers could help us get through this time. I was handed flier after flier, and after my fifth polite decline, I decided that if *one* more person tried to shove anything into my hands, I would give it to them *well well*.

I spotted the lucky lady from a few feet away just as I released the handles of my shopping cart to open my boot. The woman approached, holding a stack of papers and calling out, "Hello, Madam!"

I whirled to face her, about to let it rip, when Randy stepped coolly out of my backseat. He shot the girl a look that made her resolve shrivel. She glanced from Randy to me and back again before scampering away in search of easier prey.

I gave Randy a grateful, tight-lipped smile. "You rolled your sleeves up," I noticed. The fabric of his black T-shirt was all bunched up towards the neck, better revealing all the black swirls, skulls, lions, wings, and swords that went down to his wrists.

He shrugged. "Makes the intimidation act more effective."

Charlene and Oneisha stepped out of the car as well. Together, we transferred all the shopping into the boot.

"Thanks, guys," I said. "So we'll just offload this back at—"

Ice. Crystals formed along my spine.

Like a single organism, the girls and I turned in the same direction.

Randy started. "What's going on? Am I missing something?"

Oneisha placed a hand on his shoulder and, with her other arm, pointed to the road. Nearly everyone in the car park was already staring in that direction.

The whole world seemed to have gone quiet and cold as the spirit of a young woman marched, blank-faced, across the stretch of road we could see. Like all the other Coasters, she was naked from head to toe. By her pubescent body, I estimated her age to be fifteen, at most.

Nobody in the car park spoke or moved a muscle until the Coaster was completely out of sight. Then, one by one, we began to release our breaths. Sound and heat returned to their regular levels.

Charlene scrutinized Randy. "So you didn't feel that?" she asked. "When she arrived?"

Randy shook his head. "Feel what?"

"Your heart sinking to the bottom of your stomach," I answered. "The feeling that a cloud of darkness has settled on your head and will never go away again. The hollowness. The sense that it's a sin for the sun to rise."

From the look on Randy's face, I might as well have spoken Russian.

"You know," Charlene remarked, "there's one word that could have summed up everything you just said."

"What word is that?"

"Depression."

I couldn't respond.

The four of us filed back into the car, somber. I put the key into the ignition but didn't turn it right away.

"Guys," I blurted. "Everyone else is wrong about the Coasters. So, so wrong. I feel this pressure on my chest to scream the truth and document every single thing that's happening right now because I feel like it would serve the

Coasters somehow, but I don't have a clue how to go about it!"

I inhaled, breathless.

"That pressure that you feel, Adwapa," Oneisha said gently. "It's the ancestors speaking to you. You should listen."

I pursed my lips. "But I don't want to be one of those roadside prophets, you know? I don't want to proselytize. I don't want to draw attention to myself—"

"You could start a blog," Charlene suggested. "Keep it anonymous."

"It's a good idea," said Oneisha. "And if you're worried about it being traced back to you, I'm sure Randy has some skills that could help."

Randy blushed, so shy that it was disorienting to even look at him. "The last thing I want to do is impose," he said. "But I do want to help. Wherever you need me."

"I need all of you," I said.

Charlene reached across the gear shift to clutch my hand. "Then it's a good thing you've got us, eh?"

AN OVERVIEW OF INCORRECT
COASTER THEORIES

Published by The Coaster Reporter
Posted on December 28, 2019

Society is steadily devolving into rampant, panicked chaos after the arrival of ghostly beings from the depths of the sea, whom I refer to, on this blog, as "the Coasters." Little is known of the purpose of their arrival, despite the plethora of public theories being passed around by word of mouth and through social media. I have already published a lengthy post on the only theory I believe, which you can find <u>here</u>. This post is a broad overview of all the other theories I have encountered. I will continue to update the sub-pages as more theories come my way.

1. The End of Days

The world is ending, or at least, that's what all the Ghanaian aunties out there seem to think.

The Armageddon theory is the most popular public theory in Ghana, and even among its proponents, there are denominations. The majority of these interpret the Coasters as demonic manifestations, with sub-groups referring to them by different names: principalities, bonsam, and shaytan, to name a few. Some say they might be bringing a plague, a punishment from God, Allah, or the gods, for our sins.

The Armageddon minority is biased towards the Coasters as more benevolent divinities. Perhaps angels, or disciples of Jesus, come to warn us that this is our last chance to repent. Some believe that one of them might even be Apostle Peter himself. (This minority gives me hope, not because it has any weight, but because it indicates that at least a fraction of the public is willing to believe that entities from Heaven can be Black.)

Regardless, there is widespread debate about whether humanity will live to see 2020.

2. The Experiment

Many secular West Africans posit that this might be some large scale CGI experiment by Marvel or some other mega-company. The grand introduction of 4-D cinematic experience, perhaps. The Walt Disney Company, as far as I know, has not commented on the issue. Something tells me they never will bother to respond, assuming the rumors ever reach them in the first place.

3. The Conspiracies

The further one burrows into the hoax rabbit holes, the more sci-fi the theories get. Here are a few examples: American drones were sent to West Africa to spray the air with drugs, causing us all to hallucinate. Alternatively, the Coasters are all holograms, designed so that when Africans are wiped off the continent by nefarious means, there will be a virtual replacement population ready as a cover-up. According to this school of thought, we are only seeing the Coasters this early because something has gone wrong with the projectors.

You can follow the subpage links for more details on specific theories or navigate to the Coaster Theories category on the top-level menu.

P.S. It's worth mentioning that whenever the

Coaster phenomenon does make it through to Western media, the hoax theories are given far more airtime than the spiritual theories. Ghanaian mainstream media, however, continues to avoid the topic like the plague. There's been no news about a ban on the subject, but I know censorship when I see it.

For two straight days, I wrote like I was running out of time. *You need to tell this story*, I kept thinking. *These people can't be consigned to an invisible history, not again.*

Whenever I encountered a Coaster, I made a note of their appearance—height, weight, complexion, estimated age, any distinct features, and if Oneisha was around, their last thoughts—and uploaded it to a catalog of individual profiles on *The Coaster Report*. I would never know their names, but I had to preserve the mark of each one's presence somehow.

I organized and published every Coaster-related detail I could gather from observation, social media, and the news. I created a log of Coaster sightings, organized by country, tracking the Coasters' general progress further inland, even as some spontaneously disappeared and more rose from the ocean's depths.

Whenever I wasn't writing, I was reading or researching.

Randy proved to be a remarkably efficient assistant. All I had to say was, "Randy, can you find any research papers about slaves drowning themselves?" and almost immediately, I'd have full PDFs of books and articles saved for me in a brand new folder; or "Randy, can you find me any fiction pieces about Black people living underwater?" and in minutes, I'd have a personally curated canon in my bookmarks.

He was good with numbers and analyzing trends, which made sense, since it was his job. It was from him that I learned that the number of incoming passengers and tourists flying into Africa, the Caribbean, and South America had spiked after Christmas.

I didn't understand why everyone wasn't more adamant about avoiding these places, until Charlene declared, "It's the white people. They can see the ghosts, but the Depression doesn't affect them. If it did, I swear to you, they'd be throwing up all over themselves from the guilt."

Indeed, white Americans and Europeans treated the Coaster phenomenon like an exotic new tourist attraction—which, of course, only made the impact more cataclysmic when, on 29th December 2019, the Coasters finally found their way to the shores of South Carolina.

There was a saying I'd heard more times than I could count: "When America sneezes, the whole world catches a cold." But in those final few days of 2019, I decided that the saying didn't do reality justice. It was more like:

The rest of the world might sneeze, but no one calls it a cold until America catches it too. It was clear from the US media's reaction that they had never dreamed the Coaster phenomenon would touch them. But it had always been a matter of time before North America and Europe were drawn into the drama.

The US government reacted to the Coasters with unimaginable swiftness by shutting its borders, with immediate effect, to every predominantly Black country in the world. Americans seemed to believe that the Black people flying into the country were bringing "it" with them, whatever "it" was. Their actions set off an avalanche. Within two more days, the UK and most of Europe had closed their borders, as had much of East and South Asia.

Now that the political leaders of the global superpowers were addressing the Coaster phenomenon, our African leaders had gotten the permission they'd apparently been waiting for to do the same.

Trans-national organizations, including the AU and ECOWAS, called meeting after meeting in the space of twenty-four hours, and finally, in a coordinated move executed on New Year's Day, 2020, several heads of state delivered formal addresses to their respective peoples.

My mother, Charlene, and I watched the TV quietly as Ghana's president announced a complete national lockdown until global leaders could "get to the bottom of this unprecedented situation." No flights were to operate from any airport within the country, and no ships were to dock at our harbors. Just in case this *was* some transferable disease, all public gatherings were temporarily banned—weddings, funerals, conferences, and religious gatherings. Restaurants were to operate takeaway or delivery options only. No one was to be about town without critical business such as acquiring food or going to the hospital. At that point, none of the beaches in Ghana were operating commercially, but the president nevertheless formalized it with an order that all public beaches be closed until further notice. Soldiers would be posted nationwide to ensure these mandates were obeyed.

Similar lockdowns were announced throughout most of West Africa and the Caribbean, and less stringent ones across other countries and continents. These regulations were meant to be enforced until the cause of the uproar—in our president's terms—was discovered and appropriately dealt with.

"This is getting out of hand," my mother complained, her voice full of scorn as she stared at His Excellency's still-moving lips on our living room flat-screen. "I understand why Americans would be so dramatic about something that isn't real, but *Ghana*?" She shook her head and clicked her teeth. "Disgraceful."

I clenched my fists and closed my eyes. My mother was getting more irksome by the day. She insisted on insulting the spirits in one of the most disrespectful ways I could think of: refusing to acknowledge them.

Well, I wasn't going to stand for it.

Alright, I thought as I prepared my retort. *Here we go again*.

Following the New Year's announcements, the world and its citizens scrambled to reorient themselves. Nobody had imagined we'd be ushering in the new decade with nearly half the world in lockdown, and the first few days of 2020 were a hot mess. Everywhere you turned, there was a cascade of cancellations—conferences, concerts, and gatherings all postponed indefinitely, while the rise in video calls strained people's internet bundles.

My friends and I had all booked our return flights for 8th January, but by the 3rd, with the Coaster phenomenon showing no signs of slowing down, it was clear we'd be stuck in Accra for a long, long while.

Randy made a couple of calls to some very overwhelmed airline personnel, and a few hours later, all of our bookings had been changed to open tickets with no expiry dates.

Housing was a little trickier, but still no match for whatever spirit of fortune was ordering Randy's steps. A friend connected him with some expat who was looking to sublet his Ghana apartment now that travel restrictions had locked him out of the country. And just like that, the dilemma of extravagant hotel bills versus dumping two new boarders on top of my mother's head was resolved.

Most of the other stranded tourists worldwide weren't half as lucky.

And then there was the matter of work. Charlene, Randy, and I spent the remainder of our vacation days trapped in email threads and inconveniently scheduled calls with our employers, trying to figure out how to work remotely, account for time differences, and how the new circumstances would affect our paychecks.

"Oneisha is so lucky she doesn't have to deal with this shit," Charlene complained one evening, taking out her earphones at the end of a three-hour-long Skype call.

While she'd been busy using my bedroom desk for her meeting, I'd been on the bed, drafting up another post for *The Coaster Report*, fully aware that I had emails from Kavya—my boss, the Marginal Magazine's editor-in-chief—that I was putting off.

"I know, right?" I said. "The idea of being a self-employed visual artist with a boyfriend who dey hold sounds so good right now."

In my peripheral vision, I saw Charlene come over to the bed but didn't look up until she pushed the lid of my laptop shut.

"*Charlene!*" I protested.

"It's past midnight, Dwaps. Sleep."

"It is not!" I snatched my phone up to check the time, and indeed, it was already 12:17 a.m. "What! When did it get dark?"

Charlene slid my laptop off my lap and placed it on the bedside table before turning towards the cabinet where she'd left her pajamas. I reached for my laptop again, but she returned in the blink of an eye to snatch it right out of my hands.

"*Sleep*, Adwapa. The Coasters and your blog will still be there tomorrow."

"Fine," I grumbled, shutting my stinging eyes. "But just so you know, I'm not even tired."

I never heard Charlene's response. The next time I opened my eyes, the sun was up.

I reached for my phone and stifled a shriek at the flood of notifications. The stats on *The Coaster Report* had blown up tenfold.

By the time I sat down to have breakfast, that new number had tripled, and by mid-afternoon, the web host had given up on sending me any more notifications.

My heartbeat spluttered out of control as I refreshed the exponential graphs on my site's dashboard again and again. The comments underneath my Personal Theory posts—variations of "Omggggg" and "this makes so much sense!!!"—ignited little fires within my heart. Forget my obsessive work ethic; *this* was my favorite part of journalism: knowing that I'd brought people out of the darkness into the light and that they appreciated me for it.

All day, I couldn't keep still for longer than a minute. The terror, pleasure, and suddenness of it all fired me up.

My Twitter timeline was flooded with links from my blog! Friends and colleagues sent me direct messages, asking for my opinions on the anonymous author's take. I resisted the urge to give myself away, though. The Coasters deserved the recognition, not me. I was just glad people were finally paying attention to the truth!

In no time, *The Coaster Report* was the talk of the town, not only on social media but on mainstream media as well. Major stations from the African continent to the Caribbean, North America, Europe, the UK, and beyond discussed the contents of my blog on the news. People debated the slave theory on podcast after podcast, widening the gap between those willing to accept the metaphysical and those who still believed there was a "more rational" explanation.

Whether people believed the slave theory or not, it was out there now, pervading public discourse and amplifying Black-white racial tension around the world. I couldn't take too much credit for that, though. The Coasters did most of the work all by themselves.

GUILT AND REPENTANCE: THE COASTER EFFECT

Published by The Coaster Reporter

Posted on January 13, 2020

You may consider yourself too "rational" to believe that the Coasters are the returned spirits of formerly enslaved Africans who drowned in the Atlantic. But if you're part of the African diaspora, you know the truth is not so easy to dismiss.

For Black people, all it takes is *one* moment of proximity to the Coasters, and we feel it: that profound, core-deep discomfiture, that self-directed contempt. Unlike members of other races, the Black experience of the Coasters doesn't just stop at fear. Not even the word "awe" can do it justice. A Coaster's presence will drain us of complacency like vampires draining humans of blood. When Coasters walk away, we're left feeling like something is deeply wrong with the world and that we can't bear to continue being part of the problem. They spur us into action. It's the Coaster Effect, and it is evident all around us.

In Ghana, we can see it in the long-overdue confessionals. Over the past week, members of the wealthiest and most well-known Ga, Fante, and Ashanti clans have come forth to spill family secrets they have been keeping for generations. So many of us have ancestors who had close ties to colonizers and, thus, a hand in the slave trade. But we have never reckoned with it in the open or as a nation. Not until now.

Every day on Ghana Twitter, there are links to new petitions full of demands to re-name local boarding school houses that were named after colonizers, or motions to raise national memorials to honor the drowned. For days, there has been an outpouring of tweets from Francophone Africa railing against colonial taxes.

Internationally, protesters are vandalizing monuments of former colonial officers, racists, and slave traders. Some are even going as far as to paint them in feces or hurl them into water bodies (a very poetic gesture, all things considered). People are taking to the streets in the USA, despite social restrictions, to protest institutional racism. A few days ago, the hashtags #HonorTheAncestors and #BlackHistoryMatters started trending and never stopped.

The UK is a curious case. Despite it being one of the countries with the fewest Coaster sightings, the Black British population is causing some of the most significant ripples in their society to date. There has been at least one instance of public flag-burning, and several universities have had to suspend lessons in response to what the media terms as "disorderly behavior" on the part of some students.

The Coaster Effect is inspiring a new wave of pro-Black posters, social media posts and graffiti all around the world. Thousands of people are changing their profile pictures to show solidarity. The Black Power fist is becoming an increasingly popular icon for bumper stickers, storefront windows, and more, as people search for new ways to express their mounting emotions

It would be much more beautiful if it didn't

feel so tragic - if we could shake the feeling
that, at the end of it all, none of it will ever
be enough.

My mother walked into the dining room to find me typing
on my laptop. I barely looked up from my screen, thinking
she would just pass by. Instead, she came to a halt directly behind my chair. My fingers continued to fly, but my
shoulders stiffened.

These days, I preferred to steer clear of my mother entirely, but Charlene was on a work call upstairs, and I
couldn't afford to be distracted. Kavya was pressing me
hard about finishing this #HonorTheAncestors article for
The Marginal, which I'd been procrastinating in favor of
covering the same topic for *The Coaster Report*.

"Hm!" my mother goaded over my shoulder. "Number
one slavery historian."

I said nothing.

"Or are you now calling yourself a time traveler since it's
fiction you believe in?"

Keep it cool, Adwapa, don't satisfy her.

"Anaa w'adane fortune teller?" she continued, placing a
hand on the back of my chair and stepping back. "Sɛ, you
say you can talk to spirits?"

"Mummy, *seriously*!" I snapped. "I'm not even asking

you to believe anymore. I'm just asking you to leave me alone!"

"How can I leave you alone when I'm watching my only daughter turn into a madwoman in my own house?" she shot back.

I sprang up and whirled on her, my face level with hers. "I thought I had a mother who knew how to accept what she can see with her own two eyes."

"Ehn, and me, I thought I raised a sensible, God-fearing woman, not a superstitious simpleton!"

"*Argh!*"

"Adwapa!" Charlene's yell from upstairs sliced through my fury. At the same time, my phone screen lit up with a video call from Oneisha.

I left my mother standing there and picked up my phone. Oneisha's pixelated face formed on my screen while Charlene's feet drumrolled on the wooden staircase. At the foot of the stairs, she paused, her eyes wide and frantic. A video played on the phone in her hands. She held it out to me, saying, "Adwapa, I think we've unlocked a new level."

I watched a few seconds of the video—an older man in a wheelchair, babbling away in something that sounded like both Wolof and Twi, with his pupils rolled up so only the white of his eyes showed.

My lips curled into a grimace, and goosebumps formed on the flesh of my arms. "Is it dementia?" I asked.

"No," came Oneisha's voice, tinny from the poor internet connection. "The ancestors have begun to use some of us as mediums."

"What?"

"Possession, Adwapa!" Charlene exclaimed. "People are getting possessed!"

Oh, *shit*.

Chapter 3

OUR BODIES ARE NOT ALWAYS OUR OWN
(A Description of the Coaster Possession Process)

Published by The Coaster Reporter
Posted on February 2, 2020

A few weeks after their first recorded appearances, many of us still struggle to wrap our heads around the fact of the Coasters' existence. And now, with no warning, they have managed to send the world into another level of unrest.

Some of us hate how our African uncles and aunties love to leap first for spiritual explanations for absolutely everything—but for once, they are right. Western media is doing everything it can to avoid even mentioning the word "possession." Still, it doesn't change the fact that it is happening—across my country, across the West African coast, the Caribbean, and every region in which the Coasters have appeared. Now, we know why some Coasters walk into homes and spontaneously disappear. It means they have chosen their hosts.

There is no obvious rhythm to the possessions. One moment, someone is going about their day as usual; the next, their eyes roll back into their heads, only to roll back down a heartbeat later, wild and crazed, with a dead person's spirit looking through them.

If you've witnessed a few possessions, either in person or through videos, you might notice that possessions seem to infuse the Coasters with more than just corporeal power. They develop an almost exaggerated liveliness as if they can neither spread their limbs wide enough nor talk fast enough. Each speaks in African language dialects that are centuries outdated, with smatterings of colonial languages here and there. Words like "captain" and "ship," in what I believe to be Dutch pronunciations, come up often. So does the Akan word "abrɔfo," which, in this context, naturally implies "white people." The spirits speak with a frightening urgency, which doesn't help those of us trying to understand them, especially with the language barriers.

Once a Coaster inhabits a living person's body, it becomes an involuntary (at least on the part of the host), long-term partnership. Following each corporeal takeover, they retreat into the background, leaving the living person to their body until the next takeover. However, the hosts, when they are restored to active consciousness, insist they do not sense any other presence within their minds or bodies.

Each time a Coaster possesses a living human for the first time, there is a period of bewilderment—at the clothes, the people, and the surroundings—which adds to the panic of their already unintelligible speech. In subsequent takeovers, they gain slightly better control over themselves, and they use that control to pour their hearts out to whomever, if anyone, is present.

From the little that can be deciphered, their stories are always about their lives—the latter and most horrific parts. It is both a burden and a mercy that we can barely understand them. The Depression that settles on every human host and their household when the Coasters are active is emotionally taxing enough.

I have been trying to identify whatever trends I can regarding the possessions. So far, only one "pattern" has emerged: the selected hosts are almost always old. It is rare for anyone under fifty-five to be taken over by a spirit. Often, it is the hosts' caretakers, or younger kin who record and report the episodes. It makes me wonder, is there some threshold for the spirits, an age below which one's body becomes inhospitable to the drowned? Beyond this observation, I struggle as much as anyone else to make sense of the randomness.

In terms of frequency, takeovers are so un-
predictable that various governments, including Ghana's, have released official mandates stating that "any affected persons"
must stay home as much as possible, particularly if they have jobs on which people's
safety is dependent (surgery, driving, etc.).

As disoriented as the world is now, I am
grateful that the impact on the Black diaspora has been somewhat cushioned by the
fact that so many of us had already retained,
for centuries, the indigenous knowledge that
our bodies are not always our own.

I had made the banku too thick, and, in my laziness,
hadn't chosen a strong enough utensil to stir the dense,
starchy mass in the pot. And yet, either pride, stubborn-
ness, or both, stopped me from doing anything about it
until the plastic ladle snapped in my hands.

On the other side of the kitchen, Charlene yelped, "Yie!
Are we safe?" That typical Ghanaian response to sudden
sounds was something she'd picked up from all the time
she spent around Ghanaian diasporans in the US.

But not even her attempt at levity could pierce through

my dour mood. From the way I was acting, you'd have thought a Coaster was releasing waves of Depression right from the middle of my damn kitchen.

I sighed. "I should have used one of the wooden ladles."

I moved towards the kitchen door, but Charlene intercepted me with a protective swiftness. "I know where they are," she said. "I'll get it."

I could have pushed back, but I didn't. She loved me too well to send me back into the lion's den that was my living room, where the unchained beast known as my mother had probably already thought up a new way to strike out at me.

Tensions between myself and my mother were at an all-time high. I had always known her to be arrogant, but conceitedness and cruelty were two completely different things, and she had drifted quite far toward the latter. Lately, she went out of her way to disrespect the Coasters in front of me, as though riling me up was her new favorite sport.

She was now spending her day off from work watching some meaningless Hallmark movie. The drawer that held the wooden ladles was directly in her line of sight. If I stepped into it, she would almost certainly spit out some callous comment, and that would be it for the afternoon. But today wasn't the day I wanted to find out whether banku could get burned.

No sooner had Charlene left the kitchen than the heaviness of death clouded the atmosphere. The TV was still on, but I could no longer hear it. My insides had gone cold, and my heart was suddenly ten times heavier.

Charlene and I rushed towards each other at the same time, nearly colliding in the dining area. We held eyes for several seconds, too shocked to say a word.

There was no physical barrier between the dining and living rooms, meaning my mother had an unobstructed view of us.

"*Mtchew*," she sucked her teeth loudly. "What has gotten into you people?"

In a flash, every last emotion in my body was wholly overshadowed by fury. I whirled to face my mother, heat pulsing in my veins.

"No, Mummy, not today," I growled. "You are *not* going to lie to my face and expect me to pretend I believe you, *not today*!"

My mother stared at me with a mixture of shock and offense that I'd dared to speak to her so brazenly. But before she could say anything sarcastic, vicious, or infuriating, I continued, "You felt the atmosphere change just as much as we did, and if you want to pretend like you don't know what it means, then let me tell you. It—"

My heart stilled at the same time as my tongue. A fourth presence had entered the house. *Our* house.

I looked out through the window into the small compound, and there she was, walking through the closed gate like the metal was nothing more than a sheet of air. She was a little shorter than the average Ghanaian woman, her height and build similar to Charlene's but not quite as stout. She had thick eyebrows and a roundish face. The translucence made it hard to gauge, but she appeared to have a darker complexion than everyone present. Her hair was cropped close, Ghanaian secondary school style. That was about as old as she looked—perhaps between fifteen and sixteen, and, of course, completely naked. Coarse hair covered her crotch, and her pubescent breasts were so firm they barely moved as she walked.

Oh my God, there is a Coaster in our house, I thought. Even the voice in my head was deadpan—too many emotions to properly process anything.

Strange how easy it is to assume that something that happens to thousands of people will never happen to you; how unquestioningly you can believe in your own exceptionalism.

The formerly enslaved woman walked through the wall and into the living room. My mind and body went numb. I wondered, with detached calm, whether it would hurt to have my body taken over by a dead person. I imagined my consciousness being folded into a tiny drawer in the back of my head somewhere and an entirely different being rewiring every neuron until my current self, Adwapa, became a distant memory to my own flesh.

The young Coaster's emotionless countenance didn't

help matters. At least when someone approached you with clear, malicious intent, your self-preservation instincts kicked in. But the Coasters had the opposite effect: they were as thoroughly paralyzing as a spider's venom working within its prey.

Closer and closer, she came, until she was smack in the middle of the living room. And it took me until then to realize that her ghostly, bare feet had never quite been headed in my direction.

My breath caught. But there was no time to do anything except watch my mother's eyes, which had grown wide as saucers, roll back into her head as the spirit grafted onto her physical form.

All the feeling returned to my body in a crash. I rushed to my mother and held her down with my palms on both of her hands and my feet on top of hers. It was a good thing the armchair was comfortable, because a first-time possession would likely involve spasmodic thrashing.

And so it began—a fit full of strength I'd never guessed my mother's body still held.

The Coaster looked at me through my mother's eyes with an animalistic fear that pierced me so sharply that I nearly lost my grip. I didn't even want to think about the context of the last time she'd found herself restrained like this. It made me feel unforgivably filthy, but I couldn't let my mother get hurt. So I held on for several minutes until the thrashing and the screaming subsided.

Once I was sure that she wasn't going to harm herself, I let go slowly, one limb after the other. The Coaster in my mother's body was panting, and there was still a wildness in her eyes that wouldn't fade for some time yet. But she was no longer looking at me like I was her captor.

"Hello," I said carefully. "My name is Adwapa."

At first, I wasn't sure the Coaster had heard me, but then she opened her mouth and took a deep breath. When she released it, a torrent of Asante Twi came out, too thick and fast for me to understand a word.

I stood there dumbly in the wake of her barrage before I got myself together. For God's sake, I should have started recording from the moment she'd arrived!

I fiddled with my phone and left the voice recorder running, placed the phone on the armchair, and began to search for my keys.

Charlene, recovering from the shock, shrieked, "Where the hell do you think you're going at this time?"

"To get Oneisha," I huffed, already halfway to the door. "Watch my mother for me. Please don't let her hurt herself. And make sure the recording keeps going."

I was gone before Charlene could form a coherent response.

Oneisha was waiting for me outside their sublet apartment building, ready even though I hadn't called, texted, or contacted her all day. She got into the car the second I pulled up, and without much ado, I swung the car around and raced back towards my mother. Randy was, according to Oneisha, packing overnight bags and would soon follow in their rented car. I panicked a little, wondering how my mother would react to an unmarried couple sleeping in the same bed under her roof. That most certainly fell under her umbrella of "wayward behavior," and as annoying as the woman could be, I was not interested in triggering a heart attack. And then I remembered that my mother was currently possessed, which, of course, helped put my other anxieties back into perspective.

Between my reckless driving and the relatively empty lockdown streets, we returned to my house in record time.

Back in the living room, I forgot how to breathe at the sight of my mother slumped, unconscious, in her armchair.

"Nothing drastic happened," Charlene rushed to reassure me. "I think she might have just tired herself out."

"What does that mean?" I asked breathlessly. I hadn't seen or heard of other hosts passing out after a takeover.

"Your mother is... very stubborn," Charlene said carefully.

"Tell me something I don't know!"

"It's almost like she was fighting the spirit inside her for control of her body. And she succeeded a few times, too. It was your mom, then the spirit, then your mom, then the spirit, and I think it all got too intense, so they just... fainted, I guess?"

I groaned. This was just like my mother: to become the only person on Earth who could even partially resist a spiritual possession out of sheer unbelief!

"Hey Adwapa, it's okay," murmured Oneisha. "I brought some things I thought might help."

From her bag, she retrieved an engraved trinket box. She clicked it open and dug through it with the solemn efficiency of a paramedic with a first aid kit.

As she strung together her talisman, she explained her choices aloud: "There are two spirits at war within your mother's body. It's like a fraught but simultaneously intimate relationship. Charoite should help with that. It's the gemstone of harmonious marriage, among other things... The Amazonite should reinforce it, though it represents a slightly different kind of harmony—an openness to truth and points of view other than your own. The Aquamarine is for calm and the ability to stay rooted in the face of conflict. And I'm just going to hold them all in with some clear quartz on both sides to amplify all the other stones... There."

She presented a pretty but very obviously D-I-Y necklace of deep purple, sea blue, blue-green, and clear stones. I fastened the talisman around my mother's neck and exhaled as her breathing instantly slowed into a relaxed, deeper rhythm.

It was at that moment that Randy walked through the front door, tentative as a child. "Umm... guys?" Randy ventured. "Not to be a distraction or anything, but am I the only one who smells something burning?"

I shot upright. "Oh my God! The banku!"

Mummy remained knocked out for a couple of hours. In that time, I managed to salvage the day's main meal and listen multiple times to the recording from the possession. As I suspected, much of it was beyond my international school, counterfeit Twi comprehension. I imagined my mother would have much better luck understanding the voice note if only I could get her to cooperate, which was very unlikely.

When she finally woke up, she very nearly gave me a heart attack.

"*ADWAPAAAAAA!*!!" she screamed, with the urgency of someone held at gunpoint.

I was upstairs, preparing the guest room for Randy and Oneisha. At the sound of my mother's voice, I dropped the pillow I was handling, with its case only halfway on, and bounded down the stairs. She had screamed my name three more times by the time I made it to her.

She stopped shouting when she saw me, but she continued to repeat my name. With each repetition, something seemed to deflate within her, and very soon, she was no longer calling my name but sobbing it.

I knelt before her.

"Mummy, I'm here. I'm *here*. What's wrong?"

"The *pain*," she moaned between sobs. "So much pain."

I placed my hands on her sides, searching for wounds or a fever. "Where does it hurt?" Charlene hadn't mentioned anything about physical injuries.

"Not *my* pain," my mother whispered.

Immediately, I understood. Even then, I still couldn't muster up the appropriate reaction. Hell if I even knew what the appropriate reaction *was*. So much had happened at once, my ability to process emotions was temporarily suspended. I said the most practical thing that came to mind: "We need to get you something to eat."

Charlene helped me set up the dining table for five, and as I worked, I pondered in silence. Twice in one day, my mother had done the unheard-of: first, to have even partially resisted a possession, and second, to have formed some mental symbiosis with the possessing spirit. How did one even reverse the natural order in that way? Spirits were supposed to enter *your* head, not the other way round—unless you were Dr. Florence Mensah.

Even Oneisha, who was much better versed in the supernatural than I was, confirmed that, after a trance, a possessed person ought to have no recollection of what had been said or done during the trance. My mother, however, not only knew some of what the Coaster had been trying to tell us, but she had also felt it. The evidence was in her eyes, which looked deader than they ever had. It wasn't the same hollowness that resided in the ghosts' eyes but a terrible, hopeless pain infused with a frightening amount of shame.

It was practically evening by the time we finally sat down to have the second most awkward lunch of my life after the one from Christmas.

The only person who seemed even vaguely at ease was Oneisha. Randy looked more or less like he'd swallowed a frog. Charlene and I exchanged anxious glances whenever my mother moved so much as a finger. But if there was one consistent thing about the day, it was my mother's repeated defiance of our expectations.

She didn't say a word about the banku despite the strong stench of burned corn still attached to it. It still tasted fine, thank God, but on an ordinary day, even the slightest mistake in my cooking would have earned me a flurry of snide comments. She didn't say a word about Randy and Oneisha's presence either, which left it to me to bring it up.

I timed my announcement carefully, waiting for her to swallow another morsel of banku before I said, in a measured tone, "Mummy, Randy and Oneisha will be staying over in our guest room for a little while to... umm... help with... stuff."

I held my breath. Underneath the tabletop, Charlene grasped my hand. We were both bracing ourselves for something along the lines of, *Do you think I'm an invalid, that you've brought two foreigners to* my *house to take care of me?*

But there was a delay. My mother looked around blankly, taking a moment to digest the information. Her eyes finally landed on Oneisha, and emotion crept back into her face. I stiffened. *Here we go...*

"You," my mother said to Oneisha, gazing at her as if she were the only other person in the room. "You are a miracle."

I— *What?*

"Your ancestors survived that," she continued. "And they kept surviving long enough for you to be born. That is a miracle!"

Oneisha bowed her head. "Thank you, Auntie. I am also in awe of their resilience."

My mother offered Oneisha an expression maybe halfway to a smile before she turned her attention to Randy. "And you," she said icily. "Where are you from?"

"*Mummy!*" I gasped, utterly horrified.

"I'm, uh..." Randy fumbled, then cleared his throat and began again. "My mom's family is from Italy, and my dad's family is from Spain. But I'm American, born and raised."

"And what exactly are you doing here in my country?" my mother inquired, inflexible as stone.

"Ma!" I gasped. "How can you talk to my friend like that?"

She shuddered and looked away. "What those people did..." she whispered faintly and retreated back into her head. While she was thus distracted, I mumbled an apology to Randy, at a loss for how to feel, because although my mother had been impolite, had I not felt the fury she was now feeling, more times than I could count?

For the next few minutes, we ate in silence, except for my mother, who merely stared at nothing, breathing softly. The next time she moved, it was to lift a hand absently to her neck, where her fingers met the gems of her talisman.

All at once, she flipped like a switch.

"Heeeeeei!" she yelled. She rose so swiftly that her chair scraped backward and clattered to the floor. "What is this juju thing that you people have put on me? Hehn? How many times have I warned you not to involve me in your silly, superstitious—"

She ripped the necklace off her neck, and the gemstones clattered to the floor. Her tirade cut off the second the talisman left her skin. She lost her breath and began to sway. Had Randy been any slower, she would have collapsed onto the floor herself. It was a good thing he'd been eating his banku with a spoon, otherwise the armpit of my mother's light blue chiffon blouse would have been stained reddish-brown with okro stew.

Randy was only just releasing his grip on her, slowly so that she could find her own balance again, when she suddenly went cross-eyed. Her eyes soon refocused, but the consciousness staring through them was not her own.

She whirled like a terrified, cornered animal, and when

she saw Randy so close to her, she went wild. Ear-splitting, wordless shrieks accompanied her frantic attempts to both rip Randy apart with her arms and kick him as far away from her as she could.

All at once, everyone else was standing, trying our best to hold her back, and by the time the girls and I got my mother to calm down and return to her own, stable consciousness, Randy was nowhere to be found. The girls and I carried her to the living room sofa, where she resumed softly crying.

Oneisha washed her hands and got to work with reassembling the talisman. "Their energies are too strong," she said, explaining my mother's swoon. "The spirit hasn't accustomed herself to lifelike consciousness, and your mom hasn't permitted herself to share her body or mind. Until she and the spirit become used to each other, they'll need the gemstones to enforce stability."

I shook my head and knelt before my mother.

"Listen to me, Mummy," I pleaded. "You've been chosen as a host for one of the spirits from the ocean. You've been hearing about the possessions on the news and WhatsApp, so I know you understand at least some of it. Some of the things you're feeling, thinking, and maybe even remembering right now are not your own. You're having a harder time than most people because of your strength. It's complicated, but we can help you. But you *have* to cooperate with us. And the first step in helping us help you is to keep that necklace *on*. Do you understand?"

She gave little indication that she had heard me.

"Adwapa," she said.

"Yes?"

"The work you are doing with your platform on the internet... It's to help them? The..."

"The Coasters? The spirits? Yes. I'm trying to help them by preserving their memories, by trying to get this part of their stories right."

"Nothing we can do will change the past." She sounded so bleak I couldn't help but respond in kind.

"No, it can't."

"But we can try to atone. We can at least *try*."

"Atonement," I agreed. Ironic that my mother, of all people, had given me the perfect word to describe my motivations. "That's what I'm trying to do with *The Coaster Report*."

"Then I will. I'll cooperate."

I exhaled. Whatever had just happened to my mother felt even more unbelievable than my first sightings of the Coasters at Cape Coast. If it lasted, it would take a lot for me to get used to.

I had never seen my mother so broken. Not even in the months after my father died. In the days and weeks following her first possession, she became so utterly unrecognizable that the word "disorienting" didn't even begin to cover how it felt to witness it. I called the hospital and informed them that, in compliance with governmental mandates, my mother would be taking an indefinite leave of absence from her job.

In the meantime, my work continued. While the world tried to reckon with this third wave of Coaster unrest, I tried to get the most out of my circumstances.

It probably sounded callous, but my mother getting possessed was like a gift from heaven dropping right into my lap. For weeks, I had been pursuing my subject, and all of a sudden, my subject had come to me. Now that my friends, my mother, the Coaster, and I all lived in the same household, I had all the tools and personnel I needed within arm's reach.

The six of us fell into a daily routine. Twice a day, we organized séances with the spirit, whose name, she eventually told us, was Gyebiwaa. Between my mother's cooperation and Oneisha's influence over the supernatural, we could control the time and location of every session. At 7 a.m. every morning, all the women in the house would converge in the living room, and my mother would get comfortable in the armchair as Charlene settled on the floor before her, ready with her laptop to press record and play scribe. Oneisha and I would each hold one of my mother's hands while she willed her consciousness to recede. As my mother concentrated on retreating, Oneisha would call the dormant spirit forth, and a few seconds later, it would be Gyebiwaa, no longer Dr. Florence Mensah, occupying the seated body.

The first few times, Gyebiwaa was nearly as agitated as she'd been on the first day. But I spoke to her as soothingly as I could, in Twi that she could, thank heavens, understand: *To wo bo, wai.* Take your time. *Yɛn nyinaa, yɛ yɛ wo nnamfo.* We're all your friends. *Wo hyɛ me maame honam.* You're wearing my mother's skin. *Kasa, yɛre tie.* Speak, we are listening.

And speak she did. I didn't understand too much of it initially, but when my mother came back to herself and listened to the recordings, she could translate much of what I'd missed in conversation.

Between holding the séances, decoding them, and transcribing them, Gyebiwaa-related activities took up a full set of working hours each day.

I remembered how, during some of my Africana history courses in college, I would return straight to my room after class and sleep for hours, sometimes even through dinner, because the content of those lessons had been that intense. On the really bad days, I'd had to excuse myself in the middle of lessons to visit the bathroom and sob for a few minutes in private. And to think all that resulted from being exposed to theory, academic research, and second-hand accounts. Listening to Gyebiwaa did not compare.

And as for how Gyebiwaa herself could handle talking about it at all... Well, no human could have withstood that unless God himself was helping them bear the load.

After a couple of weeks, when Gyebiwaa had spoken of all that she could think to speak of, I asked for permission to share her story. She was fervent with her consent, barely bothered by the fact that she couldn't fully grasp the concept of the internet, much less the idea of a blog. All that mattered to her was that her story would reach as many people as possible since she had never lived long enough to tell it.

INTO THE WATER, WHERE DAMNATION IS SALVATION
(Summary of a Coaster's First-Hand Narrative)

Published by The Coaster Reporter
Posted on February 23, 2020

Her name was Gyebiwaa. She came from Asɔkɔre—a village outside of the Asante capital—and belonged to a clan that was not ranked very highly on the social scale at the time. She was fifteen when her village was raided by abrɔfo men, aided by Asante

neighbors of high rank—the kinds of people that Gyebiwaa's would ordinarily have
looked to for protection.

Gyebiwaa was abducted during the raid. She
was broken down, whipped, separated by
force from her family, and taken to the coast,
where the real torture began.

Perhaps in a different post, I may speak of
the things they did to her, to her body, and
to her fellow prisoners, the conditions they
were forced to endure on Gold Coast soil,
even before the Middle Passage. But if you
have read any of the more graphic histori-
cal documents or visited West Africa's slave
castles, you already have enough vivid details
about what it's like to be imprisoned in a
dungeon to serve you a lifetime.

There are not enough words to describe the
experience of being stripped, shackled, and
loaded onto a slave ship. To be carried against
your will onto the open water when you have
never, until that point, even seen an ocean.
Having no clue where you are going or what
will be done with you. That combination

of terror, enforced ignorance, and an active imagination is psychologically lethal. It's almost as lethal as the physical hell of being packed with your fellow humans into a hold like sardines in a tin.

Gyebiwaa was loaded into a vessel along with more than twice the number of captives its already inhumane designers had built it to carry. And thus, when a deadly disease began to spread, there was no way to escape the possibility of contagion.

As if the panic wrought by the epidemic were not enough, an outbreak of rumors accompanied it, spreading faster than the disease itself. News was passed, imperfectly, from captive to captive, that their captors had begun to talk of running out of food and water. Indeed, the rat-sized rations that Gyebiwaa and the other captives received decreased even further.

Rumors compounded that the abrɔfo were lost and had no idea where the ship was or where it headed. That there had been a change of plans in how they, the captives, were to be eaten. Many of the enslaved had already theorized that they were being transported as food for some monsters in a land beyond the horizon. Now, they believed that their captors planned to sacrifice them to the deity that ruled at the bottom of the ocean, instead.

Once again, their fears were realized when the captors began to carry out cursory inspections, tossing overboard any captives whose health or appearance displeased them, starting with the dangerously frail, the women, and the children.

The abrɔfo made themselves deaf to the screams and protests against this new brutality. And they were entirely oblivious to something else, something which Gyebiwaa herself has a hard time explaining: the captives' specific terror of death by drowning.

To understand this thalassophobia, one must first understand how the African captives had been raised to understand death. Many, if not all, believed that death was not the end of existence but merely a passage into the realm of the ancestors. That passage, however, was rarely automatic. The success of the transition depended on a partnership between the dead, the living, and the elements of nature.

The drowned would be deprived of the food and drink offerings made by the living to sustain the dead as they journeyed between realms. They would have no clothes; assuming they ever did manage to arrive in the ancestral kingdom that Gyebiwaa calls Asamando, they would have to bear the shame of nakedness. They had been given no fabric to wipe their sweat during the journey nor money to purchase provisions on the way there. But all that was almost irrelevant when measured against the greatest abomination: that their bodies would not be buried within the earth, that singularly essential element of proper transition.

If there is any element of nature that is perilous to a smooth transition, it is ocean water. A body drowned and lost forever to the depths of the sea cannot be buried appropriately in consecrated, ancestral ground. And without the burial, the person to whom the body belongs will be disconnected, in death, from their relatives, the physical remains of whom ought to be lying beside them within the earth.

The horror of being stuck in limbo for an eternity would, in ordinary circumstances, have been too much to bear. But these were not normal circumstances, and the shrewdest among Gyebiwaa's fellow captives had noticed something incredible: the captors were *upset* about having to throw so many of them overboard. Knowledge of the white people's languages was minimal, so the Africans did not fully understand why this was so—but hardly one of them cared. They had read the tension in their captors' body language and heard how gravely they argued whenever they had to carry out their soul-damning murders.

Intuitively, several of the captives—Gyebiwaa among them—recognized the power that they held. If the crew was so reluctant to throw them overboard, then perhaps the eternal wandering of their souls was a lesser peril than whatever awaited them beyond the horizon. And yet, underneath that logic was a much simpler and more persuasive reasoning: that they would do whatever displeased their enemy, purely out of spite. If they were doomed regardless, what was one last, desperate act of defiance?

For Gyebiwaa, at least, the hatred of those white men surpassed the fear of an utterly void eternity—and that was why she jumped.

Now that Gyebiwaa's story was out, there was no more need for the rigorous, scheduled séances. But Gyebiwaa's spirit remained in my mother's body, taking over consciousness—with my mother's permission, of course—whenever she felt moved to do so. In these times, however, it was *she* who engaged *us* in conversation. She was curious about the future she had never lived to see, and what her fate might have been if she hadn't decided to jump off that cursed ship.

I tried to explain, in my halting Twi, that she would probably just have experienced many more similar horrors, but this summary would not satisfy her. She insisted on hearing the details of how Africans were maltreated in the slave colonies all those years ago. She wanted to know what had happened to the survivors and the remaining continental Africans in the following centuries, from her time until mine. She wanted to know how white people today lived with the guilt of the trade, and something bone-chilling flashed in her borrowed eyes when she found out how prevalent racism still was.

From time to time, in fiction, you come across protagonists who say melodramatic things like, *It felt like everything I'd been through had been preparing me for this moment.* Well, here I was, in real life, discovering that I was one of such melodramatic protagonists.

Of course, an undergraduate degree was not enough to make anyone an expert. Yet, I couldn't help but ask, why had God, the universe, or whatever led me to complete a major in Africana Studies, if not for this moment? Why had I become a journalist if not to serve these spirits just as I was doing now?

From slavery to abolition, to institutional racism, from colonialism to independence, and then neo-colonialism, I tried to give Gyebiwaa the most accurate summaries—which would have been a challenging enough task, even if I hadn't had to do it all in Twi. I nearly cried out of frustration sometimes, trying to find the right words to express the experience of Black people in the modern world with such limited vocabulary as I had in my mother tongue.

But Gyebiwaa was patient and studious, asking questions whenever I felt too stuck to continue. She questioned everything, including things that I had unfortunately come to take for granted, like how I had grown up on African soil yet spoke English more fluently than Twi, like the invention of "Ghana," or what year it was, or the presence of ubiquitous technology.

Gyebiwaa also wanted to know about us, the people she lived with. I did my best to play the role of interpreter whenever she wanted to speak directly with Charlene and Oneisha. Randy, on the other hand, she couldn't stand to set eyes upon. Each time he was in the room and Oneisha sensed Gyebiwaa coming out, all she had to say was, "Babe," and Randy would find some excuse to pack up and leave within fifteen seconds.

Gyebiwaa listened incredulously to Charlene's story about her family's migration from the Gambia to the US. She was stunned at the idea that Africans would, of their own volition, take up residence in a country that hated, and would once have enslaved them without question. But even more interesting to her was Oneisha's story as a descendant of people who might, in another life, have been her fellow plantation slaves.

"Wo nim sɛ," said Gyebiwaa one day as the girls and I sat together in my living room. Gyebiwaa looked at me with a curious intensity and continued, "Ɛyɛ me sere sɛ w'anyini sen me." *You know, I find it funny that you're older than me.*

I was so used to seeing Gyebiwaa in my mother's body that it took me a while to recall the physically adolescent ghost I'd seen the day she had walked into our house. For this conversation, I decided to ignore the technicalities of birth dates.

"Adɛn na ɛyɛ wo sere?" I asked. *Why do you find it funny?*

Her immediate response made my mind go blank for a second. She couldn't possibly have said what I thought she'd said. I was so astonished that I slipped back into English and screeched, "What do you *mean* I could have been your great-great-grandchild?!"

Oneisha, who had been watching us intently as we conversed, cleared her throat. I stared at her.

"Adwapa," she said softly. "There's something I've been meaning to tell you."

I continued to stare, frozen in my seat. Charlene came and settled beside me, putting her arm around my shoulder like she was preparing me for a blow.

"You were so focused on documenting her story," Charlene said. "It was emotional enough for you without adding this to your burden."

My eyes flicked from Charlene to Oneisha, waiting for an explanation I was sure I wasn't ready to receive.

"Ever since the first séance, I've felt a kinship connection between Gyebiwaa's spirit and yours."

I couldn't seem to get my tongue or brain to work properly.

"Oneisha and I talked about it," Charlene added. "We think we might have figured out how the Coasters locate and select their hosts."

"At first, I wasn't sure about this, but now I am," said Oneisha. "Whenever I'm close to the spirits, I sense within them this search for familiarity. That's what they're always walking towards. And there's nothing more familiar to them than their blood."

"It's what determines their directions from the moment they emerge from the sea," Charlene explained. "They're always walking towards the person with the strongest possible blood relation, usually the oldest living person who shares their ancestry. When they finally get close enough, they inhabit their bodies."

I could barely hear her over the pounding in my ears. Why were they only telling me this *now*?

"S-s-so..." I stammered, staring once more at the woman in my mother's body. "Gye... Gyebiwaa is my... my—"

"Auntie," said Charlene softly. "Several, several generations removed."

I'd forgotten how to breathe now, too.

Every horror I had heard from my mother's lips, every bit of torture up until the moment of death, had been experienced by someone who shared my blood! She had told it all to me, a relative she had never lived to see.

The sense of loss struck me so hard that my heart nearly broke. For all the people—all of my kin—who had never gotten a chance to exist because Gyebiwaa had been robbed, at sixteen, of the chance to become a direct ancestor.

This world! This stupid, cruel, irredeemable, shitty world!

I broke out into terrible, heaving sobs, crying harder than I had since I was ten years old.

Charlene put her arms around me, and I loved her for the comforting gesture—but in that moment, it was the flesh of my blood that I needed to feel. I got up and crawled like a child into the arms of my mother, and my great-aunt, my own distant ancestor, held me as I wept.

Chapter 4

I n my mother's house, the air seemed to have gotten lighter after all those weeks of conversation and revelation. It was like some weighty yoke had finally been lifted, not just from the atmosphere but from my mother.

More than anything else that had happened since December, it was my mother's transformation that truly cemented my belief in miracles. Everything she'd gone through over the past few weeks had sucked a lot of the spite from her personality and left her with much more empathy than I'd ever believed she could show.

Now that my mother no longer needed help being taken care of, Oneisha and Randy decided to return to their apartment, politely declining my mother's extended invitation to stay. At my mother's insistence, they came over for dinner at least twice a week, even after moving back out.

Meanwhile, Gyebiwaa's takeovers became less frequent. She always came back when she had a few quick questions or a little more to share, but never with the same urgency as before. We could go four or five days, sometimes even a week, without hearing from her. There were times when my mother claimed she couldn't feel a second consciousness within her at all.

"I think she's right," Oneisha said during a group dinner when my mother brought it up. "I can usually sense spirits, even when they're dormant. And I don't feel Gyebiwaa's presence right now."

"But wherever she goes, she always comes back," my mother told us. "Usually by morning."

I snorted. "A spirit leaving its host's body every nightfall? Where would it even go?"

"Oh, come on, Adwapa," Charlene teased. "You're supposed to be the one with the writer's imagination! They're ghosts, aren't they? Obviously, they convene at night to discuss their progress with haunting, the same way witches meet to discuss their progress with bewitching. I can't believe I have to explain all this to you!"

She rolled her eyes for dramatic effect, and I rolled mine right back at her.

"If you're perceptive," added Oneisha, "You can probably feel clusters of spectral energy when you're out on the streets late at night."

I frowned. Oneisha wasn't the type to make light of anything spiritual, and hearing her riff off Charlene's joke caught me off guard. I glanced at her curiously but was surprised to find that there wasn't a trace of humor in her expression. A chill sped from the base of my neck to my tailbone. She couldn't possibly have been serious, could she?

I wanted to ask Oneisha to explain her comment, but Randy cut in, saying, "You know, I have a feeling flights are gonna start opening back up soon. If you're following some of these economists…"

As I was drawn into discussing the latest global trends, my question was soon forgotten.

My mother was not the only person experiencing less of the supernatural these days. All around the African continent and the Black diaspora, the frequency of possessions continued to dwindle until, by April, none were being observed or reported anywhere. The Coasters had all simultaneously, well, ghosted. Oneisha remained confident that they were all still vaguely around, but there was nothing but her word to show for it.

In the meantime, the suffering capitalists took the Coasters' apparent disappearance as their cue to try resuming business as usual. Thus, after about three months of lockdown, commercial flights began to operate again—first slowly, then all at once. Conferences and concerts went back to being predominantly physical. People went home, and work went on. "Formerly afflicted persons," including my mother, were given the green light to return to their jobs. The world was quickly returning to its pre-pandemonium state.

And we hadn't learned a thing.

I'd had hope for the world; truly, I had—hope that the literal reality shift that the Coasters had caused would, at the very least, have stirred humanity's collective conscience. But I'd underestimated the racist Stooges, who were, apparently, too hard-hearted to be moved even by the Ghosts of Slavery's Past.

Some of these were the indifferent officials in predominantly white countries, particularly in the UK, who pretended to be blind and deaf to Black citizens' demands for better jobs, better pay, better treatment, education, housing, health—better lives. Others were the kind who called the cops on peaceful protesters to disband them forcefully. Still, more were the ones who continued to deliberately target harmful messages and racial slurs towards a people that was collectively grieving for their would-have-been ancestors. I couldn't understand—what made some people lash out in the offensive when the only thing demanded of them was repentance?

Black folk were in pain—the type of pain that could not be understood by anyone who hadn't felt the Depression and the overwhelming sense of wrongness that came with it. The Coasters may have left the living to our own devices for now, but the effects they'd had on the Black population remained, and there was little chance we would be lulled or manipulated back into complacency as long as this remained the case.

All around the world, tension continued to boil, with no straightforward paths to true reconciliation. The tipping point was when a particular video from England went viral.

It wasn't that the video was the most outrageous display of racism that anyone had ever seen. No, we had all that already—the histories, the hatred, the murders, the injustice—all packed into a giant bomb. The video was merely the matchstick that lit the bomb's fuse. It could have been anything—but fate had chosen this.

A passenger on a London train had recorded the video. In it, another passenger—an elderly white woman—was telling a younger Black woman that "Negroes" were a cursed race and that she ought to collect her fellow "demons" (it was unclear whether she was using this word to refer to the Coasters or the rest of the living, Black population) and return to hell, where they "clearly belonged." That encounter had nearly turned into a brawl on that train, and several people had had to intervene.

The full video was over ten minutes long, the exchange barely punctuated by the train's multiple stops and shuffling of passengers. It broke my heart to watch, but not nearly as hard as it broke the rest of the UK.

Every protest and every demonstration that had taken place before this video surfaced became like child's play compared to what erupted afterward. All across the UK and Europe, millions of Black people went on strike, challenging their allies to do the same. There were countless marches and parades and, unfortunately, too many fatalities. The youth came out in droves, and they rioted, they looted, and they burned. Fire services worked around the clock to prevent entire British cities from turning into piles of rubble. Police arrested more people than they knew what to do with—many of them teens of color—and anti-racism organizations were putting in the work to get them out of custody nearly as fast as they were taken in.

The curious part of all this was that, according to the statistics, the UK and Europe had recorded some of the fewest numbers of Coaster sightings and possessions, which should have meant fewer instances of Depression-fueled violence. As proud as I was of the Black British population, I couldn't make sense of how come the UK, of all places, had turned into the eye of the storm.

Sometimes, the most I could do was stare at my screen, muttering, "What a time to be alive."

Mainstream British media, in their attempts to downplay the impact of the revolution, decided on its own headline topic to cower under: the declining mental health of white British people. I scrolled through site after site, and all I got were vapid pieces about how stressful Caucasians had found the lockdown period, cabin fever, and all the associated pandemonium. It wasn't even news! Major channels could spend half an hour per program discussing a high-profile, white person's attempted suicide and yet would barely spare two minutes for the anti-racism demonstrations. Even when they did, words like "riffraff" and "hooligans" came up too often. Major American channels weren't much better; when they could be bothered to perform solidarity for the Black diaspora at all, it generally had the air of the snow calling the cotton white.

It was extremely bizarre that "real life" was expected to continue amid all this. I didn't fully accept the fact until I had seen my friends off—first Randy and Oneisha, and then Charlene—at the airport as they returned to the US. I had pushed my departure date back as far as I'd dared, unwilling to accept that there was nothing more to report on the dormant Coasters.

Thus, I was still in Accra when Kavya emailed me instructions for my first in-person assignment in months. By the time I got to the end of the brief, I could have leaped in excitement.

My mother came home from work to find me haphazardly throwing things into my suitcase. My room was a hurricane when she walked in.

I braced myself for the blasting of a lifetime; old habits did, indeed, die hard. But Mummy leaned against the door frame and watched me with a gaze that conveyed both confidence and concern.

"You're going to England, aren't you?" she asked.

"I am," I said. "Work assignment."

Mummy crossed her arms. "Is it safe?"

There was a period of silence in which I considered lying to appease her. But we would both be able to see right through it.

"No," I sighed.

My mother gripped the wall suddenly and leaned her head back against it, closing her eyes. When she opened them again, she was no longer Dr. Florence Mensah.

Gyebiwaa regarded me with the same expression my late grandma used whenever she told me something she wanted to make sure I remembered.

"Dua a enya wo a, ɛbɛwo w'ani no," she said gravely, "yetu aseɛ. Yɛnsensene n'ano."

I frowned, my brain working furiously to translate her words, even though she'd spoken slowly. *If a tree gets you...* Wait, did "dua" mean tree, branch, or stick in this context? *It will hurt your eye...* Ah! I had it! I'd heard this proverb before. *If there's a stick that would pierce your eye if given a chance, you uproot it; you don't sharpen its edge.*

The moment I got the translation right, my mother returned to her body. She did a double-take, disoriented.

I was disoriented, too. I didn't understand why Gyebiwaa had returned after all this time to drop a cryptic proverb on me, but I felt heavier now like my spirit suddenly weighed more inside my body. I felt burdened by everything: racism, death, suffering, the state of the world. Just thinking about how much there was to do to get marginally closer to justice was exhausting.

But by all means, I would play my part, even if it meant walking right into the eye of the storm.

My flight to England was delayed, but that was far from unusual. In fact, I couldn't remember the last time I'd taken a flight from Kotoka that had departed on time.

Sitting in the overcrowded boarding gate an hour after the plane was meant to have taken off, I scrolled through Twitter with my private account. I could tell from the timeline that something dramatic had happened in the last few minutes, but it took me a while to sift through the chaff and get to the source of it all.

At last, I came across a link to a breaking news announcement that I might have scrolled right past if I hadn't vaguely recognized the person in the featured image. The headline read: *Veronica Phillips, subject of viral video, dies aged 76.*

For a while longer, I stared at the photo in the Tweet, trying to figure out why this old white lady looked so familiar. When it finally clicked, it was like someone had squeezed all the air out of my lungs.

So many emotions raged within my chest, and somewhere underneath it all, my conscience was trying its very best to muster up the customary sorrow for the loss of human life. But my mind and emotions were distracted, hooked as they were on the minutiae of this announcement and everything it implied.

"Veronica Phillips," the headline said, like the name was important enough for any reader to recognize immediately. "Viral video," like it was any old TikTok challenge, and not the thing that had sent the country that had once colonized half the world spiraling off the edge.

The article itself was, somehow, even more incendiary.

The former schoolteacher passed away at her summer home in Portsmouth, Hampshire. Her nephew and niece, who stayed with her at the time, reported that she had been "troubled" and insisted on an unsupervised sunset walk along the beach to "clear her head." A search party, formed at the request of the deceased's surviving relatives, retrieved her body from the water near Southsea Castle the following morning.

Not a word about the racist comments that had brought her into the public eye or how she had gone to her watery grave without ever publicly repenting or apologizing for them. She had catalyzed a war, but by all means, said the media, let her rest in peace. All the outrage on the timeline finally made sense.

I scrolled some more, and my attention snagged on one of the many viral Tweets on the trending topic. "The 'racist people are just mentally ill' propagandists must be having a FIELD DAY," it read.

The most absurd thought struck me then, but I had to dismiss it immediately. It couldn't possibly have been an agenda, yet, what were the chances of this particular woman dying in what looked like another of those white British suicides right in the middle of all this racial turmoil?

The fuzzy PA system announced that boarding was about to begin.

I sighed. My spirit felt wearier than it ever had. As I clutched my passport and boarding pass, I quickly prayed that I'd live long enough for my trip to England to make some difference.

What I faced upon arrival at Heathrow was my most uncomfortable airport experience to date. The airport officials treated me like I matched the description of some wanted terrorist, searching my bags as if they expected to find bombs inside them. They spat out questions as simple as, "Purpose of visit?" with such an edge that I feared a single inapt word from me would have them shoving me on the next flight back to Accra. They even asked me to step aside so my eyes could be examined, doctor's appointment-style. They didn't explain why, but it was apparent they were trying to ascertain whether or not I was possessed. As if examining my eyes would have revealed anything.

Even when I stopped at one of the restaurants for some fast food, I felt eyes on me from the moment I ordered until the second I left. I was so frayed when I settled into my

London Airbnb that one would think I'd been traveling non-stop for a week and not just seven hours.

I was glad to finally be alone in my little rented studio, with no eyes on me whatsoever. And yet, even now, the weight that felt uncomfortably like depression refused to lift itself off me. Something was seriously wrong with me. I had never felt this worn out in my life. It was psychological exhaustion that had apparently seeped into my bones and weighed my body down along with my mind. I couldn't understand why everything suddenly felt too much to handle when I felt like I'd handled things relatively well over the last few months.

I wanted to cry, scream, or experience some sort of emotional release. Instead of doing any of that, I called Charlene. She would calm me down. Remind me of the work I was here to do. Reassure me that I was strong enough to do it.

For a week straight, I traveled from city to British city, sleeping in a different bed every night, witnessing protests, capturing footage, taking notes, and conducting on-the-fly interviews. And my God, what a brilliant generation of Black British activists there were! At every demonstration, African immigrants showed up in droves, sometimes, whole families at once, protesting together. Many of them, particularly West Africans, were eager to be interviewed once they discovered where I was from.

It was revolutionary violence that Frantz Fanon himself would have been proud of, and the hope that I rediscovered in those days of being smack in the middle of it all was unquantifiable. I could openly admit that there was a thrill in escaping whenever British police showed up with their rubber bullets and tear gas to disperse us. And it was even more of an adrenaline rush to realize that their efforts were mostly in vain. For every demonstration that was shut down, two more were spontaneously organized. If the authorities had been unaware that there were over two hundred thousand Nigerians alone in the UK, not to even account for the rest of the Black population, well... Now, they knew.

Still, after all that running around, you could have put my face right next to the definition of "exhausted" in the dictionary. Even Charlene agreed that I deserved a treat for all my hard work. So I booked yet another B&B—this time for more than one night—and then I was off to Jersey Island to enjoy an ironic working holiday of isolation and writing.

This was how I found myself on my next-to-last day in Jersey, at Plémont Beach café with my laptop before me and a half-consumed cup of coffee beside it.

Over the last three days, I had consolidated all the past week's material into a coherent long form piece on the 2020 Black British protests. Besides *The Coaster Report*, I'd never felt prouder of any project I'd ever undertaken.

Perhaps that was why I'd composed the piece so fast and so tirelessly, so that now, all that remained were finishing touches.

And yet, for all that, I'd been struggling to concentrate from the moment I'd sat down at the little booth to work. The source of my distraction was, of all things, a man!

He was seated a few tables away from me, in a corner. He'd been there before I arrived, working on his laptop. He had been siphoning my attention for so long that I'd watched him sip the last drops of his first iced latte and order another. The second now sat, sweating, on the table before him, still more than halfway full.

I released a low growl of frustration so deep within my throat only I could hear it. Why was I noticing these minute details about a stranger while he was so absorbed in his work, unaware of my presence? There was nothing particularly eye-catching about a random white man with a ginger beard and a passing resemblance to Prince Harry if you squinted right. I wasn't attracted to Gingerbeard at all, and I'd never seen him before, either—of that, I was sure.

Or was I? Some touch of familiarity pulsed steadily at the back of my skull, and it had nothing to do with the Duchess of Sussex's husband.

The assault on my mind came unbidden, as disorienting as a filthy slap.

The world around me faded to black until the only thing

that remained was that white man's face. My heart raced as I thought, *Jesus, I'm either having a stroke, or being teleported, or both.*

A new environment formed around me, though I hadn't moved an inch. I was no longer in the café, but outside, at some harbor, and the man's face seemed farther away than it had a second ago.

I realized with a jolt that I wasn't looking at the man in the café. The man before me certainly looked like him. They could have been cousins, but for the fact that the man in front of me now looked like he had time-traveled from a completely different era. That was the most plausible explanation for his breeches, the frilly neck of the white blouse beneath his heavy coat, and the ridiculous admiral's cap on his head. The cap had a complicated coat of arms on it, which must have taken some incredible expertise to draw and then sew onto the fabric. Why did it make me so uncomfortable? Had I seen it somewhere before?

I stared at the coat of arms so hard my brain felt like splitting open. My body was not cooperating with my will. It was almost as if I was trying to direct somebody else's eyes where I wanted them to go. On the embroidery, flanking the crest, were those dark, bare-chested figures in straw skirts meant to be... Africans?

My breath caught. I remembered where I'd seen the emblem before: in a textbook. This was the official logo of the Royal African Company!

I glanced to the right of the sailor man and saw, docked at the harbor, a ship displaying the red-and-white flag of the RAC. A stab of terror went through my chest. Any moment from now, somebody was going to haul me onto that ship and—

"*Hrrrrrrhhh!*"

I was choking on my saliva in a café in Plémont. Staff members gathered near my table, but none dared get too close.

Shit. *Shit.* I was causing the most embarrassing scene of my life. Every eye in the room was on me at once, and yet I couldn't stop myself from choking and wheezing. I begged in vain for the ground to swallow me up.

I knew what everyone in the café was thinking: that they were witnessing a Coaster possession. It wasn't true. I was very much in the driver's seat of my mind, at least at this moment. As for the vision I'd just had though...

My choking progressed into an intense discomfort in my respiratory system. It was something like that feeling you got when you tried to force out a sneeze that was stalling at the back of your nose. But in my case, it was more like trying to force the air out of an inflated balloon pressing against my esophagus.

My eyes were watering hard enough to nearly blind me. It was a wonder I even noticed, in my peripheral vision, that Gingerbeard had gotten up and was staring at me from a few paces away.

I let out an ugly cough—the kind that sounds like a half-retch, and where your head goes up instead of down, and your mouth looks like it's trying to spray everyone within two feet of you, like an exploding faucet.

And then it was over. Barring the mortification, I suddenly felt completely fine, as if I hadn't been on the verge of asphyxiation a mere second ago.

"Ma'am? Ma'am. Are you alright, ma'am?"

I cringed up at the baristas surrounding me. "I am... s-s-so s-sorry," I spluttered.

As swiftly as I could, I packed up my things–thankfully, this was the type of place where you paid as soon as you ordered–and nearly ran back to my B&B.

Back in my room, I paced with the nervous energy that had only heightened since I'd left the café. That cough hadn't been normal. Something intangible had been expelled from me. I felt lighter than I had in nearly a fortnight, but not the least bit more at ease. Something terrible had just happened, and I wished I could get my fingers to stop trembling long enough to call Oneisha. If there was anyone in my circle who should be having strange visions, it was her, not me.

I couldn't comprehend it. I had just seen a 17th-century slave trader in the face of a man I didn't know from Adam. What in the name of Gyebiwaa—

Holy shit. *Gyebiwaa*.

I stopped in my tracks and sank to my knees, all my

nervous energy evaporating in an instant. Warmth drained from my face. I had never, ever felt stupider.

The Coasters' navigation technology was the familiarity of blood—but Oneisha never said they could only track their *own* blood.

It wasn't just a vision I had experienced in the café. It was a memory.

I broke into a cold sweat as my brain finally connected the dots—too late—and I reflected on the last few weeks and months with a god's eye view.

I should have thought more about the heaviness I'd started feeling right before my trip to England. I should have paid more attention to British headline news, to the fact that the suicide epidemics had only begun after the UK's borders had reopened, once stranded Black people had come flocking back into the country after prolonged exposure to possessed relatives. Before all that, I should have been more suspicious of Gyebiwaa's insistence on gleaning every detail she could about race relations since the last time she had walked this earth.

Jesus. The Gingerbeard man!

Oh God, Gyebiwaa, I thought in a panic. *What have you done?*

A gut feeling told me to look out my window, and if there was any lesson Oneisha had drilled into me, it was never to ignore my intuition.

I rose, with no small effort, onto my shaky legs and

crossed to the wall. My room had a view of the English Channel—which, I recalled just then, was an arm of the North Atlantic Ocean. That damned Atlantic Ocean. I'd have thought it a sick cosmic joke if I hadn't come to see that the Coasters' plan had been so deliberately calculated.

From my window, I caught sight of a ginger-haired figure thrashing its way deeper and deeper into the sea, and there was nothing I could do but scream.

About the Author

Ivana Akotowaa Ofori is a Ghanaian storyteller. Known also by the alias of "The Spider Kid," she is a weaver of words in many forms, including fiction, non-fiction and spoken-word poetry. Akotowaa has been nominated for various awards for her prose writing. Her work is included in the Flash Fiction Ghana anthology, *Kenkey for Ewes and Other Very Short Stories*, and the Writivism anthology, *And Morning Will Come*. Writing aside, Akotowaa spends much of her time looking for excuses to make everything purple. She has been included in the *Africa Risen* Anthology 2022 (Tor.com) with her short story, "Exiles of Witchery".

Milton Keynes UK
Ingram Content Group UK Ltd.
UKHW021838270924
448939UK00010B/122